How she wanted to kiss him. Right here. Right now. Right or wrong.

She couldn't think of a better place for something she'd waited a lifetime to do. Moving closer to him, her focus dropped to his mouth.

"Holly." He shook his head.

"What?"

"This is not a good idea." His voice was rough.

"I don't know what you're talking about." But her focus remained on his lips, which had haunted her for over a decade, now a mere breath away.

"Yeah. You do." But despite his hesitation, he reached up and smoothed some strands of her hair back from her face. He caught her hair in his fist and gently pulled her toward him. His mouth touched hers, gently, tentatively... But then he drew back, making her heart cry out. He watched her, carefully, intently.

"It's just a kiss," she whispered. She could hear the pleading in her own voice.

"We both know it's a hell of a lot more than that."

Redeeming the Billionaire SEAL

LAUREN CANAN

First published in Great Britain 2016
By Mills & Boon, an imprint of HarperCollins*Publishers*
1 London Bridge Street, London, SE1 9GF

Large Print edition 2016

© 2016 Sarah Cannon

ISBN: 978-0-263-06635-7

Printed and bound in Great Britain
by CPI Antony Rowe, Chippenham, Wiltshire

Lauren Canan has always been in love with love. When she began writing, stories of romance and unbridled passion flowed through her fingers onto the page. Today she is a multi-award-winning author, including the prestigious Romance Writers of America Golden Heart® Award. She lives in Texas with her own real-life hero, four dogs and a mouthy parrot named Bird.

She loves to hear from readers. Find her on Facebook or go to her website, laurencanan.com.

This book is dedicated to
Laurel Hamrick for the endless
support and the many hours she gave
so willingly. And to Kathleen for her
patience and determination to make
this story the best it can be. And to my
closest friends (you know who you
are!) who provided so much support
when it was needed the most.

One

Watching a newborn foal rise to its feet for the first time was a sight Holly Anderson would never tire of seeing. With a few staggered steps and some encouragement from its mother, the foal located its dinner bucket and didn't have to be shown how to latch on to her first meal. The fluffy little tail flipped and turned as the warm nourishment filled her tummy.

"I thought we were going to lose this one," said Don Jefferies, owner of the mare that had just given birth with considerable help from Holly. "I've been raising quarter horses most of my life and I guess I've been lucky. I've never had to deal with a breech birth."

"They don't happen that often," Holly agreed. "Thank goodness."

"I can't say how much I appreciate you, Doc."

"Glad I could help." Holly took one last glimpse at the foal before stepping out into the hallway as Don closed the stall door behind her. She began gathering her implements, then walked to the truck and dumped them into a white bucket filled with a special cleaning solution. "I should come back out and check them both in two or three days. I'll need someone here to contain Mother. She's probably not going to like having her baby kidnapped for a few minutes."

"No worries. I'll call your office tomorrow, schedule a time and make sure someone is around to help if I can't be here myself."

With a final handshake, Holly tossed the last of her gear in the holding compartment in the back of her truck, climbed in behind the wheel and headed back to the clinic. The sun had set and twilight was quickly folding into night.

She'd finished scouring the equipment and

was rinsing her hands when the little bell over the front door chimed. Someone had entered the building. She must have forgotten to put up the closed sign again. It had been a twelve-hour day with an emergency wake-up call at seven thirty this morning, and her body was screaming for a long hot soak in the old claw-foot tub.

Drying her hands on a paper towel, she made her way through the back of the clinic, rounded the corner and stopped at the edge of the front counter. She had already turned off the overhead lights but the glow from the lab area provided some illumination. Two men stood just inside the door of the small waiting room. She immediately recognized Cole Masters, one of the three owners of the ninety-two-thousand-acre beef operation across the road. She'd grown up with the three Masters sons; her aunt's small house, where she lived now, was just across the road from their mansion on the hill. Although they were several years older, that hadn't stopped any of them from forming a lifelong bond of friendship that was more like extended family.

As to the identity of the man who stood next

to Cole, she had no clue. He must be a business associate out for the weekend. Cole and his brother Wade randomly brought people to the Circle M for a leisurely weekend in the country with horseback rides and cookouts over a campfire—by an accredited chef. Why anyone would need a professional chef to cook a hot dog over a grill was beyond her realm of understanding. To each his own, she supposed.

She didn't sense any type of tension indicating an emergency. Cole just stood there with a stupid grin on his face. It was late. She was tired. And she needed to get home to the baby so Amanda, her friend and temporary babysitter, could go home. Whatever he was up to, she needed him to pull the prank and be done with it.

"Hey, Cole," she said. He nodded. "Did you forget your way home again?"

"Ha. Ha."

"How can I help you?"

"I wanted to pick up the antibiotics for the sorrel mare that cut her foot. Caleb intended to get them but something else came up. I told him I would stop by if you were still open."

"Right. I'd forgotten. They're in the fridge. Be right back."

She slipped into the main room of the clinic, grabbed the drugs out of the refrigerator along with a few syringes, dropped them all in a plastic ziplock and returned to the front. "Here you go. Caleb knows what to do but if he has any questions, tell him to call."

"Sure thing."

Cole stood in the same place, making no effort to move.

"Was there something else?"

Cole glanced over to the other man next to him, then back to Holly.

Holly bent slightly forward and held out her hands, palms up, a silent way of asking, *What do you want?* "It's a little late for charades. I'm sorry, but I've had a really long day. How about you skip the theatrics and just tell me what you need?" She glanced at the other man. "I apologize. He gets this way sometimes."

The man shrugged, pursing his lips as though finding the situation funny. Cole's grin grew wider. "Ah, man…this is too good," Cole muttered to his friend. "We should have brought Wade."

Holly didn't know what to make of that statement. What was *too good*?

"Okay." She patted the counter. "You both have a good evening. If you don't mind, lock the door on your way out." She turned to leave, headed for the rear entrance and made it all of three steps.

"Why do you have to leave so soon, Muppet?"

Holly froze. Her heart did a tiny dance in her chest. That voice, deep and raspy. That name. Only one person called her Muppet. But it couldn't be. Could it? Holly turned as the big man with wide shoulders walked toward her, removing the Western hat that had been pulled low over his eyes. In one blinding flash the past twelve years vanished and she was looking into the eyes of her best friend.

She should have known him even if she hadn't seen his face. It was the way he moved, silently, with the grace of a cougar. It was how he held himself, feet apart, broad shoulders back, big hands at his side, ready to handle any potential threat that came his way by any means necessary.

He had a ruggedly handsome face, with high cheekbones and a sharp jaw that stood out despite a five-o'clock shadow. His hair was the same dark saddle-brown color as his brothers' but instead of a suave businessman's cut, it was shaggy, disheveled—which capped off his devilish, sexy looks. His appearance had once driven most of the county's female population crazy. The Roman nose would have given him the distinction of royalty had it not been broken due to his preference of football in his youth and no doubt some hard-fought battles on enemy lines. The cleft in his chin completed the image.

Holly knew those full lips were punctuated by dimples on either side and hid strong white teeth. It was the kind of smile you waited for. Hoped for. And when it finally came it was more than worth the wait. But it was the crystal blue of his eyes that conveyed the true power of his persona. It was as though they were lit from inside. His gaze could be as daunting as a thief at your window on a moonless night, as hypnotizing as a cobra, as erotic as two lovers in the throes of passion or, like now, it could sparkle with humor. She'd once wondered if he even noticed the second glances from people he passed on the street. Or was he so accustomed to people taking another look that he no longer paid any attention?

He was dressed in desert fatigues and a light brown T-shirt, which showed the chiseled muscles of his arms and chest to full effect. There was a black-banded watch that had more dials than an Apollo spacecraft on his tanned wrist.

In front of her stood a warrior. A US Navy SEAL.

Chance Masters had come home.

"Chance," she whispered. She reached her hand out to him, needing to prove to herself he was really here. He caught her smaller hand in his, placed it firmly against his chest and held it there. She felt his heartbeat, steady and sure, beneath the thin material of his shirt.

Tears stung her eyes and she blinked rapidly, trying to prevent them from falling while she scrambled to gain control of her emotions. He'd been her best friend, her first crush and her first heartbreak when he'd left for the navy. The entire community had felt his absence. Some, mostly the women, had been saddened by the void his leaving created, while others, primarily the parents, had breathed a sigh of relief that he was gone. But his leaving had affected everyone in one way or another for three counties around. Her older brother had once told her he wished he had a nickel for every woman Chance turned down.

She stepped into his arms, her hands encircling his lean body while he held her close and let her cry. Hot, raw vitality surrounded her, causing her senses to ignite in a fire that swept through her. After a few moments, she stepped back and wiped the tears from her cheeks. She sniffed and with a quick movement tossed the strands of hair that had come loose from her braid away from her face, determined to regain some measure of control. She pulled in one shaky cleansing breath, placed her hands on her hips and jutted out her chin with purpose. "Commander? It's about damn time you came home."

That earned her a smile. He looked down, shaking his head.

"I was about to say you've changed, Muppet. But maybe not," he said teasingly, his voice deeper than she remembered. "But no braces. No pigtails. And you seem a bit taller."

Holly smiled. "You think?"

She'd been barely twelve when he'd joined the military immediately after graduating high school, so yeah, in twelve years there had been changes. But all the change wasn't on her side. She was intensely aware of the pure animal magnetism oozing from every pore in his body; he was an alpha male in every sense of the phrase. A jolt of awareness shot through her veins, pooling in her belly, making the temperature of the room rise fifteen degrees. At least.

Gone was the swaggering teenager with an easy smile and a reputation for knowing where to find trouble, the cocky guy who was too smart for his own good. He'd been replaced by a man who had seen the world through different eyes, used his above-average intelligence for things that mattered and trained to hold his emotions carefully in check. It was all there in his face. He oozed self-confidence; his nearness and the underlying power of his physique made her intensely aware of his utter masculinity.

Easily six foot four of hard muscle, he was more dangerous than she would ever have guessed a dozen years ago. She could see small glimpses of the old Chance beneath the hard exterior but it was as though the Chance of yesterday had faded away, leaving only minute traces behind. He'd finally made peace with whatever demons had been haunting him all those years ago, making him everyone's number one nightmare. But she could tell the impatience and restless energy were gone, held tightly in check by the powerful man he had become.

"I'm so sorry about your dad." Her glance swung to Cole, including him in that statement.

"Thanks," Cole replied.

Her eyes returned to Chance. "He was so proud of you. We all are."

Chance nodded, for the most part letting the comment slide. Holly remembered there had been rumors of discord between Chance and his dad. She hadn't known Mr. Masters very well. He was rarely at the ranch. She remembered her brother once confiding that according to Chance, the man wasn't proud of anything money couldn't buy, except more money, adding he hoped when his old man died he could manage to take some of it with him because he'd never cared about anything else.

Holly stood next to Cole as Chance walked around the clinic noting the instruments, X-ray machines and microscopes. Two additional rooms were fully set up to conduct a surgical operation, and there was a separate smaller space for patients recovering from surgery. The kennel area for boarding was at the end of the hall, clearly marked by a sign on the closed door. "This is nice, Holly," he said, glancing around. "Calico Springs has needed a vet for a long time. You always said you were going to get your license and build a clinic. You're the one who should be proud."

"I had a lot of help. Kevin Grady is co-owner. I couldn't have pulled this off without him. He is a licensed vet who has wanted his own clinic for years. It worked out that I had the building, and in exchange for the use of, I could work under his supervision for my last two years of clinical instruction—the hands-on experience diagnosing and treating. And your brothers helped a lot with a loan for the equipment. But yeah, I'm glad it worked out. The hours are long, the work is hard at times, but it's fulfilling."

His eyes found hers. "I couldn't have said it better." A silent understanding passed between them. Chance felt the same way about the life he'd chosen.

His expression turned serious. "I'm sorry about Jason," he said, referring to Holly's older brother, who'd been killed in Iraq. "He was a great guy."

She nodded and glanced down, suddenly uncomfortable. "There are some days I forget he's gone. I'll pick up the phone to call him then realize…he isn't there."

Chance and Jason had been best friends since fourth grade when Chance's mother had finally won the battle for her sons to grow up in a normal environment, pulled them out of boarding school and enrolled them in the local public school. The two had hit it off immediately and remained best friends until the day Jason died. Holly imagined when Chance received the news that Jason had been killed it had been hard for him to take. Chance was closer to Jason than his own brothers.

"Listen, you're tired. I'll be here a while. We're gonna head out but I'll catch you tomorrow."

"I'll hold you to that."

Chance nodded. "Absolutely."

"And *you*…" Holly pointed at Cole. "You are so mean for not telling me Chance was home." She scooted over to give him a sisterly hug. "But I guess we love you anyway."

He just chuckled. With one last look at Holly, Chance followed Cole out the door.

Rather than drive, Holly took the footpath that extended from the clinic through the trees, over an old wooden footbridge that spanned Otter Creek and on a few yards farther to her small house. *Chance is really home.* He'd made it through how many deployments? She could only imagine. And he looked good. Better than good. It had been so many years. What had he done all that time? Fight wars? Dodge bullets? Probably accomplished feats that even if he could talk about them, she wouldn't fully comprehend. Things she was no doubt better off not knowing.

She picked up her pace. Amanda Stiller, her good friend for many years and her temporary babysitter, might be anxious to go to her own home unless she'd become engrossed in something on television. At fourteen months, baby Emma could be a handful, and Holly was anxious to relieve Amanda.

But Amanda was a TV junkie and Holly had a satellite dish with some three hundred channels to keep Amanda occupied, so it was a good arrangement. Amanda often preferred to crash on her sofa instead of making the drive into town, especially now that she was in between jobs. She was an RN specializing in surgical care, and the local hospital had been forced to lay off half of its medical staff, but assurances had been given they would be recalled as soon as budget demands were met. Amanda saw it as an opportunity to catch up on her second job: being a couch potato.

Holly stepped through the back door and heard the sound of one of Amanda's favorite shows. The background music foretold something bad was about to happen. Seconds later there was a gunshot. A woman screamed and another began to sob. This was Friday night. So that meant Amanda was watching *You Can't Hide. Good grief.*

"Who died?" Holly asked as she dropped her bag into a chair.

"That old witch, Ms. Latham. She got shot."

"Again? Are you sure it isn't a rerun?"

"It's not."

"I wonder who did it this time." Holly tried to contain the sarcasm. The fictional character had been shot, stabbed, choked and drowned more times than Holly could count and she didn't regularly watch the show. Amanda and half the town were more than willing to bring her up to speed on who had done what, then ask if she had a guess who was behind it.

"I'm betting John because he wants to marry her daughter and the old biddy had it out for him. I mean, whoever pulled the trigger, she had it coming. She was up to something. I could tell. If somebody didn't shoot her, she'd have really hurt John sooner or later."

Holly clamped her mouth shut and headed for the kitchen. Amanda got so caught up in her soaps that she talked about the characters as though she'd just watched the evening news. Dear old Ms. Latham would be back in one form or another. Just today, the owner of one of Holly's patients had remarked that the actress who played the crotchety old biddy had signed a contract for another year. But Holly wouldn't spoil it for Amanda.

"Are you staying over?"

"Yeah. This sofa is way softer than my bed at home. And I still don't have cable or satellite. All I can get is the local news and weather, and nothing exciting ever happens around here."

"You do know there are stores that are only too happy to sign you up for three hundred plus channels?"

Amanda shrugged. "I'd rather be out here with you guys than sitting in that apartment alone. David won't be back for another month. Oh. Almost forgot. I promised Emma we would go see the kites tomorrow."

"Out at the lake?"

"Yeah."

"I'd forgotten it was this weekend. That should be fun. She'll enjoy it. It's my Saturday to work but it's only half a day." Holly looked over the counter into the den. "Amanda, you don't have to go to the park. You do so much for us anyway."

"Please. I want to or I wouldn't do it."

"Thank you. I'll close the clinic and get out there as soon as I can."

The commercial ended and Amanda turned back to her program. Holly made herself a pimento-and-cheese sandwich before heading for the baby's room, eating as she went. Emma was asleep on her back, her little arms splayed out on either side of her head. The silver-blond curls surrounded her face like a halo. She bent over the bed and placed a kiss on the small forehead.

Regret again filled her heart that Emma would never know her mother or father. Jason would have made a terrific dad. She hoped the pictures she had of her brother and the few she'd obtained of his wife would help Emma relate to them when she was older.

Every minute she was forced to leave the baby in someone's care, guilt hit hard and heavy. Often on the days she worked in the clinic, Emma stayed with her, either behind the counter or in the small office just off the lab, in her playpen. But on those days of ranch calls, like today, even knowing Amanda was taking care of her didn't help reduce Holly's self-reproach.

Jason, her brother, had been killed two years ago in Iraq when an underground IED exploded, taking out his patrol vehicle and everyone on board. His death had brought on their father's fatal heart attack. Four months later Jason's wife died giving birth to Emma, making the baby an orphan before she ever opened her eyes. Now all they had was each other. Emma was safe and protected, and until the baby was grown and could make her own life choices, Holly would do everything in her power to ensure it stayed that way.

She switched on the little night-light in the corner of the room and set her sights on the bathroom and a long hot soak in the tub. After undressing and filling the tub, she turned off the tap, settled back into the hot water and let her mind drift. It immediately went to Chance. He'd changed, but then didn't everybody in twelve years? Cole had told her a couple of months ago that Chance had been wounded during a mission. She'd felt her blood turn cold as the shocking news had set in. No further information had been forthcoming, and all Holly could do was cling to the old belief that no news was good news. When Chance hadn't appeared at his dad's funeral, she'd just known something horrible had happened. She'd carried that fear for days, refusing to bother Cole or Wade during their time of grieving. If they got any news—good or bad—surely they would tell her. Then tonight when Chance walked into the clinic, the relief had been so overwhelming all she had been able to do was hold on to him and sob like a baby. He must've thought she'd turned into a total and complete dork.

Bath over, she pulled on an old blue T-shirt, checked on Emma once more and fell into bed. She smiled in the darkness. Chance had finally come home. That thought ran through her mind over and over again as though daring her to believe it. She'd almost reconciled herself to the idea he might never return. In a way, he hadn't. At least not the old Chance she'd known all her life. When she'd hugged him, it was like hugging a warm pillar of marble. The small scar on his jaw added to his intensity. There was a fierceness in his eyes. His face denoted wisdom far beyond his years. Cole had once mentioned Chance was thriving in the navy, moving up in rank much more quickly than others. Once he set his mind to do it, she wasn't surprised.

The rabble-rouser he'd been in his youth, the solitary bad boy, had been reshaped into a soldier: the best this country had to offer. He was big and dangerous and no doubt very capable. But while they may have redirected his spirit, no one would ever control it. It was that streak of wildness that made him who he was. His brothers didn't have it. Just as their brown eyes would never be a hot icy-blue like Chance's, their spirit would also never rival his. Chance had always been different, always found his own road. He'd found his place in life, a place he was meant to be. Unfortunately, it required him to put his life on the line each and every day, and that was something Holly wouldn't let herself think about.

For the first time, she knew why the older girls had gone a little crazy those dozen or so years ago. It was not something Chance did purposely. It was just part of who he was. It was in his stride, his voice, his touch—in the way he presented himself. It was the way he looked at a woman, making her very much aware of her own femininity and what he could do with it.

Just being in his presence for a few amazing moments, she'd felt that silent challenge to come to him. If she did, instinct told her she would never be the same again. Before, she'd been a child and sexual attraction wasn't even in the picture. Chance had seen her as a little sister. Now, as an adult, the look of male want in his eyes reinforced the fact that she was a woman in every sense of the word and he knew it. And her body had responded accordingly.

With a moan she rolled over onto her side. Despite the years of dreaming he would someday come back and she would be *the* one in his life, she couldn't imagine this was her wish coming true. Reality had long since become her guide. Chance was home because he'd been wounded and needed a place to recuperate. Then he would once again be gone. Twelve years and her life had gone on. She needed to let go of the little-girl fantasies. The world had changed and so had they. It was sad in a way, but the happy memories from her childhood, made even better with the passage of time, would always remain close to her heart.

She couldn't help but wonder if Chance would still enjoy working with new colts and riding out to check the fences or rounding up the calves for annual inoculations and electronic branding. Horses used to be his passion. More than likely he hadn't had that opportunity in a long while.

He had also loved the river that ran for miles through the ranch land. Before Emma, she would often ride out to the place he loved the most, sit on the boulder that jutted out over the rushing water and try to imagine where he was and what he was doing. As the years rolled past, like fallen leaves carried out of sight by the waters in the stream, she'd had to accept she might never see Chance Masters again.

But he was here. She would see him. *Tomorrow.* She wouldn't think any further into the future than that. She absolutely would not, on the day of his arrival, consider how hard it would be when he left yet again. *He is here.* She could touch him, talk to him face-to-face and have an opportunity to make some new memories.

She had to wonder how he was doing up in the big house. Suddenly being thrust into the lap of luxury probably wasn't comfortable to him. While some dreamed of having even a tenth of the wealth of the Masters family, Chance had always shrugged it off, never wanting to talk about it. Holly imagined that the living accommodations he'd had for the past few years were vastly different from the mansion. Was he sleeping? Was the fact he was at the ranch making him restless? Or maybe he normally kept different hours, awake at night and asleep during the day.

If she didn't get to sleep pretty soon, she might

go down to the barn. Anything beat tossing and turning in this bed. And if Chance Masters couldn't sleep, the barn was where he would be.

Two

"I'm not saying you *have* to leave the SEALs and transition into the corporation," Wade defended himself. "I'm just saying I think that's what Dad would have wanted."

How in hell could Chance argue about something neither he nor his older brother could prove or deny? His father had said nothing about time frames the day he'd told Chance he was washing his hands of his youngest son and his outrageous behavior. He'd strongly suggested Chance join a branch of the military before he ended up in prison. So he'd enlisted in the SEAL program. He very much doubted his dad cared if he ever laid eyes on his youngest son again—and he never did—let alone expected him to slide into an executive position in the billion-dollar conglomerate upon his death. Apparently Wade hadn't been told everything that had gone down that day in their father's office. And tonight at least, Chance wasn't about to enlighten him.

Wade had taken to the role of CEO in the corporation as easily as downing the first cold beer after working the cattle chutes on a hundred-and-ten-degree day. As chief financial officer, Cole had pretty much had the same experience. But corporate America had never appealed to Chance. Not when he was younger. And damn sure not now.

"It's always been a family business," Wade continued. "When his brother died, Dad carried on by himself. And he did pretty damn good. I think it was always his intention that his sons would join him."

The kitchen staff entered to remove the empty dinner plates, inquire about dessert and offer more coffee. Chance nodded and pushed the twenty-two-carat gold-rimmed cup toward the man standing to his left. He knew the family saga. He didn't have to hear it again. It was painfully ironic to him that their dad had devoted his entire life to building a dynasty for a family he'd all but ignored for the sake of building it. Wade could call it what he wanted, but that was screwed up. And from what Chance could see, Wade was going to be just like their father. He just hadn't as yet met a woman who would put up with it. It was a bit disconcerting to think of the type of woman who would.

"Why don't you take a day and fly into Dallas with us while you're here." It didn't sound like a request to Chance, but he let it go. "Take a look at some facts and figures and get an idea of what Masters Corporation, Ltd., is about. What we do. What we are trying to achieve."

Wade seemed impervious to the fact that Chance already had a company. It was the US Navy. And for the life of him, Chance didn't know how to get that across without an out-and-out clash that might leave one, or both, wounded inside. Now was definitely not the time to go there.

"No problem," Chance agreed and stood up from his chair, ready to get out of this room and check out something that did interest him: the ranch. "Name the day and let's do it."

It wasn't that he had no concern or curiosity for the business. He would be glad to have an inside look at what had provided income for all the Masterses exceedingly well for three generations. He just doubted he was ready to put down his weapon and pick up a pen and a calculator. Still, he owed Wade enough to let him have bragging rights. Wade had always been there for him so a trip into Dallas was the least Chance could do.

Wade reached out, offering Chance his hand, which he readily accepted. "It's good to have you back, little brother. Don't think too badly of me for wanting to keep you around a little longer."

"Oh, I absolutely understand. You're still ticked off that you never could beat me in a game of chess."

Wade's smile was immediate. "Something I intend to change."

"Yeah? Good luck with that."

Wade laughed and Chance took the opportunity to leave on a high note. He'd known this visit would be hard. He just hadn't realized he'd be drawn into such a nettle-filled quagmire. His emotions about his father dying were screwing with his head; he wasn't sure if he should feel saddened or relieved. Wade was determined to make him part of the corporation, pushing him to leave the military. And heaven help him when he was near Holly. His body had hardened just saying hello to her earlier in the clinic. He was mentally at war between wanting to know this very sexy, beautiful young woman a lot better and staying well clear of his best friend's little sister. It hadn't been a full twenty-four hours since he'd arrived at the ranch and already she had him in knots.

It was dark when Chance ventured outside. The fresh night air felt good. He inhaled the scents of pine and freshly cut alfalfa. He was determined to not give in to the stiffness in his knee where the surgeons had removed a bullet and tried their best to repair bone fragments and torn ligaments. He'd never made it through a full thirty-day leave without being called in early for immediate deployment. But this time, he knew that was not going to happen. He rubbed his left arm, hoping it might relieve the dull pain that lingered from the injury to his shoulder. The last mission had taken out two of his men and left him with a couple of brass .45-caliber souvenirs. The first bullet had missed his heart by millimeters, so it could have been a hell of a lot worse. But the rounds from the AK-47 had still managed to do enough damage to kick his butt and put him in the hospital for a few weeks. The round that blew out his knee had been the real zinger. That was the injury that could change his life.

The attending doctor hadn't been convinced Chance could get back to 100 percent. For the missions Chance was trained to do, it was crucial. The doc had been up-front with him. Further medical evaluation was warranted and he was sending the case to the medical evaluation board for review. A soldier might be physically able to return to a full life as a civilian, but the injuries could prevent him from performing his duties, especially the duties of a SEAL.

Chance had been told straight up this might result in a medical discharge, something he was not willing to even think about. What in the hell would he do if that should happen? The issue was not about money, but the way he lived his life. He'd found his place. Hell, he'd *made* his place, worked harder than most men to attain it. He wasn't ready to step down to a trainer position or become a desk jockey, but at least he would have those options. Hopefully.

He was grateful for the time he had here with his family. He loved his brothers and he didn't want to cause any hard feelings. If that should happen he would carry the regret with him a long time. But their roads had gone in different directions. He respected what they had accomplished. He hoped they would do the same.

He spotted a dull light on the next rise that seemed to flicker behind the branches of the trees as they caught the evening breeze. The main barn. As schoolkids, he and Jason had spent hours in there, grooming and cleaning tack—not because they had to but because they'd both enjoyed it. Holly was usually tagging along or hanging out with them. Busy hands provided a good environment to talk. When they weren't in the barn they were in the saddle, riding the hills, checking fences, enjoying each day without considering that eventually it would all come to an end. It was strange. Only after seeing Holly tonight did he feel like he was truly home. But still, it was not the same without Jason.

His brothers had told him Holly had only one year left before she received her veterinary license and that she had a clinic across from the ranch entrance. But they omitted how much she'd changed, and for a guy who'd seen pretty much everything life could throw at him, he'd been unprepared for the vision standing before him. He's been blown away.

He'd always thought her older sister was beautiful and had been surprised when she'd agreed to go out with him back when they were high school seniors. That one date was all he'd needed. Karley wasn't the kind of girl he usually dated. She was a breath of fresh air in the purest form, and he was anything but. He'd never asked her out again. When she'd called, he'd shut her down.

He knew she'd been hurt, but he'd needed to make sure there was no further contact between them. Through the booze- and drug-filled haze, he'd done the right thing. Now he was again facing temptation with her younger sister, but this time it was far worse.

Holly was utterly feminine, almost fragile in the way she moved, like a ballet dancer on stage, and conveyed an innocence wrapped up in a tough persona. He was intrigued from the second he'd stepped inside her clinic. She was nothing remotely close to the scrawny little kid who'd followed him around the ranch, asking one question after another, ranging from why frogs hopped to where the clouds went on a clear day. He had often wondered when she found time to breathe.

She was still slim, but maturity had added some appealing assets. Her hair fell in a long, flaxen braid down her back. Her fine features were timeless; the delicate arch of her brows enhanced soft, honey-brown, almost golden eyes. The small button nose was now refined, adding to the delicate balance of her face. And heaven help him, her lips were made to be kissed. He let out a long breath and tried to gain control of his body, which suddenly had a will of its own.

In the years he'd been away, Holly Anderson had matured into a remarkably beautiful woman. Chance abruptly realized where his mind was headed and brought it to a halt. That type of awareness was completely inappropriate. Holly had always been like a kid sister to him. Theirs was a special friendship, a unique bond, and he would not do anything to change that. At least that was his steadfast intention.

Without conscious thought he walked across the natural stone courtyard around the pool, bypassing the twelve-foot-high waterfall, to the wrought iron gate between open pasture and the estate grounds.

Like the main house, the huge barn structure utilized a lot of natural stone beneath log beams reaching up some fourteen feet high to support an A-frame dark green roof. Accents of the same mossy color were added to the cross boards in the doors and the shutters outside each stall. Inside the massive structure, there was a lobby with trophy cases and a sitting area. To the left, a hallway with mahogany wainscoting led to the office on one side and two wash and grooming stalls on the right. Straight down the main aisle of thirty-six stalls, there was a grain room, blanket closets, tack room and two separate oversize stalls for foaling. To the right, there was a three-bay equipment garage. The indoor arena, with its elevated viewing area, was only slightly smaller than the outside arena.

Soft nickers welcomed him. The vibrant scents of cedar and pine shavings, alfalfa and leather soothed him. The barn, for all its amenities, seemed smaller than he remembered. He strolled down the center aisle, glancing at the horses in their stalls, some still munching their evening grain or pulling a bite of hay from their overhead rack. They were all bred to be the best and they appeared to fulfill that expectation. Their silky coats shone, even under the dim nighttime lighting. Alert and curious, some were excited at the prospect of leaving their stall for exercise in one form or another, regardless of the time, day or night.

He reached the open door to the tack room, and the scent of all the leather and the oils used to clean and condition the various pieces of tack lured him in. Western saddles sat five deep on the twenty-foot-long racks. Bridles covered one wall, halters another, with various other tools and grooming equipment in the floor-to-ceiling cabinet in the corner. He noticed an English saddle at the end of one of the saddle racks. That was new. You sure couldn't work cattle with it. But then a lot of the wrangling was done on four-wheelers today. He reached over and picked it up. It was light, less than half the weight of a Western saddle. It was probably there to appease some guest who came out for a weekend and didn't care for the Western riggings.

Back out in the central hall, he walked to the far end of the barn to an open area where hay for the stalled horses was kept. He sat down on a bale, leaned back against the wall and gazed at the sky. He missed this. He'd done plenty of night maneuvers, but the last thing he thought about then was gazing at the stars.

He drew in a deep breath and blew it out.

Until a decision was made regarding his ability to perform his job, all he could do was walk the tightrope and keep his fingers crossed. He'd been assigned to see a civilian doctor while he was here. Hopefully he could add some positive input. But Chance had a sickening feeling in his gut that his life as a SEAL was over. It was how he'd deal with the news that caused the turmoil in his head. He was thirty years old. A lot of guys dropped out of the program by now. No doubt all of them wished they had the opportunity Chance was being given by his brothers. But he didn't want to go there. If his brothers were content with the corporate side of things, good enough. But he wanted no part of it.

Holly again flounced onto her back, staring at the ceiling fan's blades whirling silently in the darkened room. This was so not working. She was tired. She'd had a long day. But even after a soak in the tub she couldn't go to sleep. Her mind refused to shut down. Glancing at the clock, she calculated she'd been lying in bed tossing and turning for almost two hours. Sleep was not even in the neighborhood, let alone knocking at her door. And she knew the reason was because Chance was home.

He was probably up in the big house with Wade and Cole. It was well after midnight. They were probably asleep. Even if they weren't, she wasn't about to disturb them on Chance's first day home. *But.* What if he wasn't with them? What if he was restless and couldn't sleep either? What if he'd wanted some air? There was only one place he would go at one o'clock in the morning.

Swinging her legs off the bed, she grabbed a pair of jeans and a T-shirt. A quick peek into Emma's room assured her that the baby was sleeping soundly. Finger-combing her hair, Holly grabbed her phone and slipped into the tennis shoes by the back door.

"Are you leaving?" Amanda mumbled, half-asleep but still glued to the television.

"Couldn't sleep. Just going to take a walk. Have my cell if you need me."

"'Kay."

Holly stepped outside and began jogging toward the main barn. If he wasn't there, at least she could run off some restless energy. But if he was there, she didn't want to waste a second that she could be spending with him.

The night air was cool to her skin with a hint of moisture. The creatures of the night continued to chirp as she jogged down the path, across the bridge and onto the main ranch road. She passed the driveway to the big house and finally reached the barn on the far rise.

The large outside double doors were open. The center hall had been swept as usual and there was no sign of anyone inside other than the current four-legged residents. She took a quick peek into the office. Finding it empty, she ventured down the hall, glancing inside the grain and tack rooms. No sign of Chance. Her shoulders dropped in disappointment. She turned around and started walking back the way she'd come when she heard a sound. It sounded like a snore. She stopped. After a few seconds, there it was again. It was coming from the far end of the building. Curious, she headed that direction. Sure enough, in the open area on the left, intended for keeping a monthly supply of hay for the horses that were stalled, two long muscled legs were propped up on a bale of hay. As she stepped closer, she knew it was Chance. He was sound asleep, his hat pulled down over his eyes. She should just go and let him sleep.

She really should.

She chewed her bottom lip and glanced at the stacks of baled silage. He could always go back to sleep. This was too good to pass up. Pulling a foot-long strand of hay from a nearby bale, she checked to make sure it had the dried seed-pod on one end before slowly creeping toward him. Crouching on her knees, she reached out and touched the wispy end of the straw against his nose. He stirred and batted at his face. Holly had to work hard to stifle a giggle as she reached out again.

In less time than it took to blink he grabbed her arm, propelled her over his body and down onto the hay with him on top, one hand around her throat, the other holding her hands above her head.

Time stopped. His face was mere inches from

hers, his look fierce, his eyes hard and deadly. She didn't know if she should try to speak or just remain absolutely still. She'd heard of soldiers with PTSD having bad nightmares. But Chance's eyes were open, glaring and focused on her.

"Chance?" She said his name, barely over a whisper. "Chance, it's me, Holly."

"I know it's you," he assured her, his voice low and angry. "I know what you were doing. And I know you came damned close to getting yourself killed."

"Sorry. Lesson learned," she squeaked. But he wasn't letting her up. His granite body was pressing her down into the hay, making her intensely aware of the absolute power and total control he commanded. He released her neck, but still held her hands above her head. His eyes were mesmerizing, entrancing, and changed her need to escape into an almost desperate desire to stay. Her fright faded, turning into something else entirely. She could feel part of his body becoming more rigid, more unyielding, and she fought the overwhelming temptation to press her hips against him. She threw her head back, closing her eyes as she battled the need for him. She could smell the sweat from his body. All sounds around them stopped. Then it was too much. She was burning and she knew Chance was the only one who could make it stop.

She felt his warm breath on her face and her eyes opened, her gaze falling on his lips, full and enticing, only inches away. Absently she pulled her bottom lip inside her mouth, moistening it with her tongue. In the dim light she saw his face harden, the muscles of his jaw working overtime. In spite of his anger, she craved to know what his kiss would feel like. Twelve long years ago when she'd jumped into his arms and kissed him good-bye, she'd just been a kid. Her action had taken him by surprise and he had immediately set her away from him as shock and aggravation covered his face. But she'd held on to the memory even though it hadn't been enough. Not nearly enough. It only provided a childish dream she'd carried in her pocket all this time. Now he lowered his head, his mouth coming closer while at the same time she felt the solid ridge of pure adult male begin to throb.

* * *

"*Goddammit*, Holly."

With an abrupt move, he rolled off her and onto his feet. Disgust at himself for almost kissing her waged war with the frustration that he hadn't. It wouldn't have stopped after a few kisses. She was too damn enticing and it had been too long since he'd felt the pleasures of a woman. *Damn.* Gritting his teeth, Chance strove for control. Holly was more than just another available female. He would not take her like this, even if she asked. Not in a barn. Not in a bed. Not anywhere for any reason. He sucked in a deep breath and held out a hand to help her up.

She scrambled to her feet without acknowledging him then sent a glare in his direction. He probably should apologize, but he had a tough time saying he was sorry for something he didn't regret. She appeared decidedly uncomfortable, looking in any direction but at him. She'd offered herself and he'd rejected her. But dammit, didn't she understand? She wasn't a one-nighter, a onetime roll between the sheets. She was so much more than that.

"Use a small bit of common sense."

"You sure do wake up grumpy."

Grumpy? He'd call what had almost happened a lot of things. Grumpy wasn't one of them. He dropped his head and let out a sigh. Rubbing the back of his neck, he contemplated how to explain why he appeared *grumpy*.

"Holly, I spend most of my time, night and day, in areas of the world—in situations—where the only way you stay alive is by use of a sixth sense. It's awareness. And you can never turn it off. If someone sneaks up on you, you have to assume it's the enemy, and we are trained, if he's that close, to take him out and ask questions later. If you don't assume it's the enemy, in all likelihood you'll be dead before you figure it out. It's an automatic reaction."

"I didn't know."

Chance nodded. "Now you do." He rested his hands on his waist. She hadn't commented on the fact he'd come perilously close to permanently changing their friendship, and as long as she was feeling insulted, he might as well get it all out. "And there is one other thing I feel the need to mention. I will not have sex with you. We will *never* have sex. You are a friend. A very special friend. You are also Jason's little sister." He drew in a deep breath and blew it out. "I will not touch you in that way. Ever. It would end what we have now and I don't want to lose that." If she had so much as raised her head a quarter of an inch, touching those amazing lips to his, they might be having a completely different conversation about now. Or no conversation at all.

"Fine by me," she huffed right back at him. "What makes you think I would ever want to have sex with you anyway? Of all the unmitigated gall. Your arrogance defies description."

"Is that right?"

"Yes," she hissed. "I don't even find you interesting…in that way."

"Sweetheart, make no mistake. Our feelings greatly differ in that regard. I want *you* until it hurts. You are without doubt the most beautiful and the sexiest woman I've ever seen in my life. But I will not touch you, even if it kills me. And it very well may. Now, why are you here? What did you need?" He couldn't keep the frustration out of his voice and no doubt sounded a lot more surly than intended.

She adjusted her stance and the look on her face was somewhere between insulted and incredulous. "What did I *need*?"

"You woke me up, so you must have a reason." He barked out his explanation then waited for an answer.

Her arms hugged her body in a protective stance as she glared at him. Silence ensued.

"What?" He enunciated the question. "Has it become a secret all of a sudden?"

She narrowed her eyes in anger. "I was just trying to place who you are. Because you're sure not my friend Chance."

He shook his head and huffed a sigh. "Holly... look. I'm sorry, okay?" How long had it been since he'd apologized to anyone?

"I didn't *want* anything, *Commander* Masters. I didn't expect to be attacked. I didn't come looking for a good time. And I sure didn't anticipate a lecture on how not to wake up an ill-tempered, arrogant grump. When did you get so bossy? You used to be nice. Sorry I bothered you." She spun around and marched toward the exit at the front of barn.

"Holly."

"Good night," she snapped without turning around.

Just let it go. You're asking for trouble if you don't let her go.

"Holly." *Shit.* He ran a hand over his face. "Wait."

She slowed her steps, finally stopping, but she still didn't turn around. Her hair fell in gentle silver-gold swirls past her waist. Small bits of hay clung to the silken strands. He watched as she slowly turned around, saw her chin jut out, displaying the stubborn streak she'd had since she could talk, and silently cursed himself for getting into this situation. With that angelic face and a body *Playboy* would kill to add to its centerfold collection, he knew he'd just made a big mistake. Another one. His body was still erect and throbbing, ready for action of a different kind that had nothing to do with the battlefield. Spending too much time around her he could easily lose his mind. Or find himself in a whole lot of trouble. Maybe both.

"I...I couldn't sleep," she said finally, her voice soft. "I guess it's because you're home." She huffed out an embarrassed laugh as though she now thought the idea was completely lame. "I considered maybe you might be out here and could use some company. I thought we could talk. Like we used to. Sorry I woke you up."

Chance muttered a string of silent curses, all aimed at himself. He could feel all the little spears of warning jabbing his body and mind, each one screaming *No!* as he nodded, sat back down on the old blanket he'd found in the office and patted a corner, silently inviting her to join him.

"I would like your company. I'll try to be nice." With a shift in body language, Holly approached him, moving the loose strands of hay around and fussing over the makeshift bed like a hen building a nest. When she finally had her spot the way she wanted, she sat down and grinned up at him. She was radiant. She smelled of some kind of berries, probably her shampoo. It was nice. Not all flowery like what some women used. He could feel the slight heat of her smaller body next to him as she relaxed against the wall.

This was a very bad idea.

"So have your brothers hit you up about quitting the SEALs and coming home permanently?"

He wondered which of them told her about their little plan. "Wade?"

"Cole." She smiled. "I take it that's a yes. And let me guess. Might your answer have something to do with you being out here in the barn?"

"You know, Naval Intelligence could use your talent."

"It isn't that I'm snoopy," she countered. "All that much," she qualified. "People just like to blab. Especially men."

"I'm going to let that pass."

"That might be wise." A frown covered her face, an indication of sincerity.

"So tell me about your clinic."

"It's there. You saw it. We've had this conversation. I'd rather talk about you."

"I'm sure I'll regret this...but what about me?"

"Exactly."

She sounded pleased that he understood. He

didn't understand a damn thing except the need to adjust his pants. He turned his head and looked down into her eyes. Their faces were separated only by the width of their shoulders. He watched as her eyes dipped to his mouth. And stayed there. Her teeth were so white against her slightly open lips. His ability to remain indifferent dropped to below 2 percent. Give or take. With jaw-clenching determination, he looked away. "What can I tell you?"

When she didn't immediately answer, he turned back to her, noting how she'd again lowered her gaze to his mouth.

"I'm not exactly sure how to put it." She chewed her lower lip. Then let it slide from between her teeth until her mouth was again slightly open. Moistened. Full. Ready for kissing. Her soft honey-brown eyes looked directly into his.

"Is it hard?"

Three

Chance froze as a flare of heat once again surged to his groin. He cleared his throat and tried to weigh the question. He'd been around the men in his platoon too long. They all tended to break the tension and stress by intentionally putting the wrong connotation on something another said. This was Holly. Especially after what just happened, it was better to be safe.

"Is what hard?"

"What you do. For a living. Being a SEAL." She looked down at her hands, fiddling with a piece of straw. "I know you guys are the best, but even then, sometimes… Sometimes bad things happen. Like…what happened to Jason. I know you were hurt. Wade told me. I hear about an accident in Iraq or Afghanistan, like a chopper going down or our men being killed by some hidden bomb, and it's all I can do to take another breath. I know what it's like to get that phone call from a near hysterical wife who is calling to tell you your brother—her husband and the father of their baby—is dead. I can't imagine what it must be like on the other side. To actually see someone killed or badly injured."

He felt her struggle to not break down.

"After Jason… It became so real. It was no longer just a news report that happened to someone else. They could be talking about you. I pretty much held my breath every time they announced another casualty or bombing involving our guys, only relaxing when Wade didn't call to tell me anything after a few days."

That surprised him. He'd never considered that Holly would follow the news reports from that part of the world out of concern for *him*. He sensed she needed to know more than she'd probably been told. "It's a job, Holly. One that needs doing. I try not to think any further than that. I trust my team. I know they've got my back and in return they have confidence in me and we get it done. Sometimes bad things happen. But that's true wherever you are, whatever you're doing." They all prepared for that moment; they all knew the next breath could be their last, especially in SEALs. But he refrained from saying that out loud.

She was quiet for a long time.

"I wanted to write to you." She shrugged. "Especially after Jason was killed. Wade offered an address." She shook her head. "I was afraid I would say something that might cause you to lose your focus."

"Nah. You should write. I'd enjoy hearing from you."

She looked up at him. "Really?"

"Well, yeah."

She settled back against the board wall and he felt her relax. One of the horses nickered; another answered.

"The horses are always ready to go. Night or day. I love their spirit. So eager to be saddled and taken on an adventure. I think they enjoy it as much as the riders do."

"I would have to say you're right. The biggest problem I used to encounter was holding them back when they wanted to tear ass and run."

"Do you think you can still do it?"

Chance had to get a grip on this. There were so many ways this question could go.

"Do what?"

"Ride a horse." This time she looked over at him, frowning. "What did you think I meant?"

He shrugged and hoped she would let it go. Distraction was the key. "Hell, yeah, I can still ride. It's like a bicycle. Once you learn…"

"Isn't that what they say about sex?" she asked. "I suppose it fits both scenarios."

Sex? Did she bring that up on purpose? He glanced over and saw the look of pure innocence on her face. *Nah.* "What do *you* know about sex anyway?" It was out before he could stop it.

The cool look she gave him didn't require words. But she answered anyway.

"Really. Are you honestly going there?" A look of disbelief covered her fine features. Her mouth was open in awe. Again. "Chance, I'm twenty-four years old and a year shy of being a doctor. I probably know more about sex than you do."

He absolutely refused to take up that challenge. "I didn't mean it that way."

"What *way* did you mean it? That I'm just a dumb little girl who never left the farm?"

"Your intelligence has never been questioned. I know you're smart," he murmured, adjusting his jeans in the most unnoticeable way he could. "You always have been."

"Okay. Well, that kinda narrows the options."

Chance didn't like where this conversation was going. He didn't want to think about Holly in another man's arms let alone his bed. *Hell.* It was none of his business. Holly was an adult and she could date whom she wanted. But he still didn't like it. Those bullets had done more than knock out his knee and shoulder. Apparently they had severely screwed with his head.

"Who is your boyfriend? Maybe I know him." *Safe subject.*

"Don't have one. Once the clinic caught on, I barely had time to breathe. That's when we hired

Jolie to run the office, take the calls, set up the appointments."

"You said Kevin Grady is the co-owner?"

She nodded.

"I remember him. Red hair? Thick glasses?"

"Yeah." She nodded and smiled. "You should see his kids! Anyway, he has the experience but couldn't handle the workload by himself. I had the land and the old house that was left to me when Aunt Ida died. And that old masonry building sitting empty. So we formed a partnership. So far it's working. There are two high school boys who work weekends and evenings, cleaning and caring for the boarded animals. Even then it's still hectic at times. Right now we are all struggling to learn the new computer system."

"You'll get there. Look at how much you've accomplished already."

"I guess. I owe a lot to your brothers. They fronted the money for the equipment. We're making payments but I'll be so glad when I've paid them back.

"Hell, I doubt if they're worried about it."

"So when are we going to saddle a couple of horses?"

Chance hesitated. In actuality, he wasn't so sure he could still swing up into a saddle. His right knee was still healing. It was mended enough that he could hide the tendency to limp. And the left knee took the brunt of the weight when he put his foot in a stirrup. Maybe he could manage without doing any more damage. "I don't know. I think Wade is expecting me to spend some time in Dallas but that probably won't be until next week."

She let her head fall back against the wooden wall and grinned like a cat that had just found the key to the milk vault.

"What?"

"I have something I want to show you while you're here. Something I've recently gotten into. I'll bet if you give it a try it will have you flat on your back and begging for mercy in about eight seconds."

Mother of God. He wasn't going to ask. He. Would. Not. Ask.

"Aren't you going to ask what it is?"

"No."

"You sound grumpy again." Her eyes narrowed as she gave him the once-over. "You must be really tired. I know you've experienced a lot of emotions today. I'll wait until you get your strength back and show you. Give you a live demonstration. It's easier than trying to describe it anyway. I guarantee you're going to think I've gone absolutely wild-child crazy. But I love it. You get into this rhythm and feel all that power beneath you, pushing you up and slamming you down, and know you control it…ah man, there's nothing like it."

He pinched his eyes closed and took a deep breath. He could feel her looking at him. For the life of him, he didn't know how to tactfully respond.

"Can we change the subject?" He cleared his throat. Why had he ever decided to come to the barn?

"Sure. Are you in pain?"

"No." *Yes.* But not in a way he could do anything about at the moment.

She nudged his arm playfully. "What do you want to talk about?"

He hadn't found one safe topic of conversation so far and he was quickly running out of ideas. When he'd thought about coming back to the ranch to recuperate, he hadn't envisioned this. He hadn't considered how Holly would have grown and matured into someone he would love to know better. A lot better. And thoughts like that wouldn't cut it. He needed to clamp down on his wayward thinking and he needed to start right now.

"How about on Sunday we grab a couple of horses and disappear for a while? I'll tell Wade we will go into Dallas later in the week. I'd like to see how things have changed on the ranch."

"That sounds great." She yawned. "Maybe then I can show you my new passion."

He let his head bounce against the back wall. *Goddamn.* This was so messed up. He needed a smoke. Or a beer. Or both. The last time he'd seen Holly she'd been a child. For some reason she'd taken to him and he'd not been able to stop her from following him around the ranch, first with her brother there, then the few times when he wasn't. She'd been too young to take a hint and he wasn't about to hurt the feelings of a little ten-year-old by telling her to get lost and leave him alone. She had persisted and not only had he begun to enjoy her presence, he'd missed her when she wasn't around.

She'd been a cute kid, smart, never hesitating to speak her mind and not caring if she insulted someone in the process. He'd respected that. Especially in one so young. It was just over fifteen miles between her home and the school, so hanging out with her friends and classmates had rarely been an option for her, even after she'd joined 4-H. He'd definitely been like a second big brother. That status forever changed the second he'd stepped inside her clinic earlier tonight.

He felt Holly snuggle into his shoulder, her hand falling across his waist. It wasn't long before the sounds of the night were the only things he heard. He leaned farther back against the board wall, scooting down in the hay, absently smoothing his hand over her long silky hair.

How many times over the past ten years had

he sat for hours against a stone wall, his senses alert to any sound out of the ordinary? The desert air had been dry, dusty, with a smell like something was rotting, the nights cold, the landscape harsh. In his mind he'd always walked through the plan of attack they would carry out just before sunrise, going over it in detail time after time. Recently, though, images of this ranch had pushed strategic preparations out of his head. The lush green pastures, the smiling faces. And sometimes he'd begun to wish he could come home to exactly this, although he hadn't really envisioned Holly snuggled in his arms. But that made it even better.

He had to question what was changing inside to make him start thinking of home after twelve years. Twelve years next month. At that time he would sign up for another three-year stretch if the medical evaluation board didn't determine he was out of the military forever.

Chance heard footsteps and looked up to find Wade walking in his direction. The smile on his face and a slight shake of his head said he wasn't surprised to find Holly asleep in his brother's arms.

"Just checking," he said in a lowered voice. "You both okay?"

"Yeah. I was just about to walk her home."

Chance stood up, then gathered Holly into his arms. She weighed next to nothing. A couple of tentative steps told him his knee could do it.

"Her house is behind the clinic a few yards. There's a path and light. You'll see it. It was her aunt's old house, if you remember."

"Thanks."

Walking to the front of the barn, Chance stepped out into the semidarkness. Holly had tucked herself into his arm, her head resting on his shoulder. He could feel her soft breath against his neck. When the smell of berries infused the night air, it was intoxicating. She was intoxicating.

A sudden sense of being home wrapped around him like a heavy fog. He could see only the road beneath his boots and the gentle face of the woman who slept in his arms. Drawing a deep breath, he inhaled the familiar smells of the ranch and heard the sounds of nature that stirred in his mind memories he'd carried since forever. He felt uplifted, although exactly what caused it, he didn't know. For the first time since he was wounded—maybe further back than that—he didn't feel the restlessness that speared him on each and every day. He felt at peace.

Stepping off the gravel road onto a well-worn path, he heard the water running in the stream seconds before he felt the cooler temperature inside the tree line. He smelled the rich, raw earth. Then he heard the hollow sound of his footsteps as he crossed the wooden footbridge that had existed long before he'd discovered it. He skirted the clinic, and with one last glance down at Holly, he stepped up onto the small patio of her home and opened the door.

If the woman watching TV in Holly's house thought it strange to see a man step inside with Holly in his arms, she hid it well.

"And you are?"

"Chance Masters. And Holly is fine. Just asleep."

"That way." The woman pointed to her left. "Down the hall on the right."

"Thanks."

He laid Holly on her bed, pulled off her shoes and covered her with the blanket. He had to get a grip on this. Fast. Less than twenty-four hours back on the ranch and he was putting her to bed and fighting the desire to climb in with her.

Holly was a beautiful temptation. But Chance knew it would be unethical to come on to her, especially when his future was not set in stone. Some women were in it for the sex and were okay with no promises of forever. When he disappeared on a mission, the women he dated just found someone else. He couldn't see Holly in that light. She was as special now as she'd ever been and she would expect more from him. Maybe a lot more than he could give.

He needed to find something that would guarantee that distance was maintained between them. With every breath Holly reminded him he was a man. Every muscle in his body tightened, making him throb with painful need. The vision of Holly beneath him, the delicate features of her face glowing in mindless captivation of their sexual joining, her eyes locked to his as he moved inside her.

He had to stop it. Now.

But even so, the innocence of their friendship was forever gone. Whether a good thing or bad, there would be no going back to the way they were.

Four

Holly awoke to Amanda shaking her shoulder. "It's almost eight. Are you opening the clinic today?"

Holly moaned, nodded her understanding and sat up.

"You slept in your clothes?"

Looking down, Holly realized she was fully dressed except for her shoes. "I guess I did."

"And you fell asleep in Chance Masters's arms? Are you like kidding me?"

Holly nodded. "We were talking and I guess I did fall asleep." And Chance had brought her home. More than likely she'd been in his arms.

It was typical of her rotten luck that she couldn't remember it. "We've known each other as far back as I can remember. He and my older brother were really tight."

"If I was with that man, the last thing I would do is fall asleep." Amanda sipped her coffee. "Go. Have your shower. I'm preparing Emma's cinnamon oatmeal. How long is the hunk staying, and is he married, engaged or involved?"

"I don't know. I don't think so."

"Mmm, mmm, mmm," Amanda muttered as she returned to the kitchen. "That is one fine man."

When Holly emerged from the shower, Amanda had already dressed Emma and was helping her eat breakfast. Holly paused to kiss the baby good-morning and gave Amanda a grateful hug before she left the house.

A quick peek around the corner of the clinic to the front parking area showed no cars in the lot. After entering the building, she put on some coffee, turned on the computer and scrolled through the appointments for the day. There were eleven scheduled and none was serious: annual vaccinations, a horse for pregnancy confirmation and a pig that limped. Probably stepped on a nail or cut its hoof in some way and it had become infected. Not a biggie. But hogs took everything to the extreme. One touch in an area they didn't want you to touch and they would scream. And scream. And scream. And they were loud. The town should find a way to use them for storm warnings. Everyone in the county would hear it.

She poured a cup of coffee and headed back outside to the far end of the building where there were four pipe-and-cable pens. Inside two of the pens were two mares that were due to be picked up today. They were recovering from founder brought on by too much spring grass. Some horses could handle it. Some couldn't. But both mares were looking good, back on their feed and ready to go home. And with no boarders scheduled, the clinic would be closed.

It was shaping up to be a perfect weekend. She could make it to the Kite Festival and enjoy the afternoon with Emma. And then Sunday maybe she and Chance could go riding. Just as she stepped back inside the building, the little bell over the front door chimed and she welcomed the first appointment of the day.

Following the curving road through the trees, Holly slowed the truck as she neared the parking area for the Calico Springs County Lake. It wasn't a huge lake, but covering several hundred acres, it was big enough for skiing and fishing tournaments. Its ever-growing popularity attracted families from Dallas on summer holiday. They had recently added more camping grounds and additional shower facilities. She found a parking spot and hopped down from the truck. Kites in every shape, size and color filled the sky. Amanda said they would be near the B section of the campgrounds and Holly headed in that direction.

A lot of the people brought their own food. Ice chests and containers of various sizes filled every available space on the picnic tables and lined the brightly colored quilts that had been spread out over the green grass. The aroma of hickory and mesquite wood filled the air as people grilled hot dogs and hamburgers. There was face painting, and vendors sold an array of food and sweet temptations along with lemonade, souvenirs and, of course, hundreds of kites and plenty of cords of string to fly them.

Holly caught sight of Emma as Amanda knelt before her holding a pink kite. Jogging over to them, Holly swung Emma into her arms, giving her a big kiss that made her giggle. Emma pointed to the colorful paper *birdies* in the sky and couldn't contain a squeal of excitement before Holly put her down. Taking her hand, they made their way through the crowd toward a grassy knoll that bordered the lake. Amanda held a pink kite and a spool of string while Holly attempted to tell Emma what they were going to do with it. The baby's eyes were wide as she sucked on her first finger and looked at the sky.

"Kite," Emma said, pointing to the object in Amanda's hands.

"Yeah. That's right." Holly grinned. "It's a pink kite, isn't it?"

"Pekite."

"Are we going to fly it up in the sky?" She pointed up at all the other kites, bobbing and twirling on the breeze.

"Fye!" And Emma pointed up, mimicking Holly's actions.

"Okay, you guys ready for the launch?" Amanda asked as she held the kite over her head and let out some string. "Here we go."

With near perfection, the kite caught the wind and took off, rising as fast as Amanda could let out the string. Emma laughed and pointed to the kite. "Pekite."

"Are you ready?" Amanda asked.

"Ready for what?"

"Blake Lufkin just spotted you." She nodded her head in a direction just behind Holly. "Yep. Here he comes."

Holly closed her eyes. Why wouldn't the man take no and just find someone else? "Wonder what he wants now."

"If I had a guess it would be that he's going to ask you to go to the rodeo. Isn't that coming up in a few weeks?"

Holly shook her head. "I've got to work. They're setting up a tent for me next to Doc Hardy."

"I wouldn't tell Blake or you'll have company all night."

"Pekite." Emma pointed to the water. Holly looked in that direction and saw the kite floating precariously close to the lake's surface.

"Uh-oh," Amanda said to Emma before running hard in the opposite direction. The kite hesitated, dipping even lower before a gust of wind sent it soaring again. Amanda returned to where Holly stood, still laughing.

"I want to go back to the couch, the air-conditioning and the TV," Amanda said. "Too much exercise for this girl. Oh. Here he comes. Think I'm gonna go and find something cool to drink." She shoved the cord of string toward Holly's hands.

"No. Amanda, pull the kite in. We're all leaving." *Crap.*

"Hey, Holly," Blake said in his annoying nasal tone as he stepped up next to her.

"Hi, Blake." Holly forced a smile at the cowboy. "How are you today?"

"Good, thanks. I just got off work. Thought I might find you here."

Holly nodded. He might be a nice guy, but there was nothing appealing about him. Over the past few months, it had started to become a problem. He would show up at the clinic, materialize in the aisle of the grocery store, even come walking into the dry cleaners, offering to carry her clothes. Every time he'd asked her out, she'd turned him down. There was nothing about him that she wanted to know better. She thought by now he would have taken the hint.

"Pekite," Emma told the strange man and pointed up.

"Yeah. That's a fine kite." He grinned at Emma. "Here, let me take that string for you, Amanda."

"No. Really. That's okay." She gripped the cardboard a little harder. "We were just leaving."

"Then, let me reel it in for you."

Holly switched the baby to her other arm and watched as Blake took over the honor of official kite reeler and waited for the inevitable question to come. Amanda made her escape.

Where was Chance when she needed him?

If someone had told him to go fly a kite with even a small degree of seriousness, Chance would have thought they were crazy. He'd honestly never seen a sight like this. Kites everywhere. The vividly colored paper contraptions with long tails flying against the stark blue sky, all reflected in the serene surface of the water, were such a contrast to what he'd become used to for over a decade, he couldn't quite get his head around it. There was color everywhere. It was like waking in the Land of Oz.

He'd been told in town that Derek Brown, a longtime friend, would be out at the lake. Chance decided to track him down, wondering at the same time if he would know him if he saw him. They'd told him to look for a silver Ford truck with spurs hanging from the rearview mirror. It would most likely have a boat trailer attached. Or a red fishing boat, if the crappie weren't biting. The guy who'd given these directions had failed to mention the Kite Festival.

As Chance made his way through the maze of erratically parked cars and trucks, he kept his eyes out for anyone who looked somewhat like Derek.

"Well, I'll be damned." A voice behind him sounded very familiar.

Turning, Chance looked into Derek's familiar face as he stepped from behind a tree. He hadn't changed. Not one damned bit.

"How're you doing, my man?" He pulled Chance to him in a manly hug of friendship. After a couple of slaps on the back, Derek stepped back and just looked at his old friend.

"When did you get in?"

"Yesterday."

"I'm sure sorry about your father."

"Thanks."

"So how long are you here?"

"I'm not really sure. Maybe a month."

As they continued to talk and catch up on what had transpired since the last time they had been together, a flashing motion a few yards behind Derek caught Chance's eye. A woman's long blond hair had come lose from its stretch band and she was struggling to hold it back with one hand while holding her baby in the other. It was a small family: a man trying to reel in a kite, a baby laughing in the arms of its mother.

Nothing unusual. Except the mother looked a lot like Holly.

Chance refocused on Derek, nodded at what he was saying—something about his eldest son— then gazed again at the couple. The woman had turned and was pointing up to the kite, her face now clearly in Chance's field of vision. It *was* Holly. Who was the guy? More important, whose baby was she holding? They looked like the typical happy family. Holly hadn't said anything about being married. In fact she said she didn't have a boyfriend. So who was flying her kite? About then she looked in his direction and made eye contact.

He once again focused on Derek. It was none of his business whom Holly saw or what she did in her life. He had no right to even speculate. He refused to acknowledge the feeling of his stomach plummeting to his knees.

"If you have time," Derek was saying, "I'd like you to meet my family."

"I'd like that," Chance told him honestly. He needed to be someplace else. *Any*place else. "Are they here?"

"Yep. My wife—you may remember Mary Beth Carter? She's grilling some burgers as we speak. Have you had lunch? There's one with your name on it."

Chance nodded. "That sounds good. If you're sure she won't mind."

"She'll be tickled to see you. It's just over this way."

Chance would enjoy spending some time with the friend he'd come to see. And he would not give Holly a second thought. He could keep his eyes on the ball during a reconnaissance mission where he led his team deep into the heart of enemy territory time and time again. He should have no problem focusing on lunch with one of his good friends.

But by the third time Derek asked him if he'd heard what he'd said, Chance knew it was time to give it up. He shook Derek's hand, nodded to his wife and thanked her for the great meal, promising Derek they would get together again before he left. He apologized for his inability to focus, blaming it on jet lag. As he walked back to the parking area, he couldn't prevent his eyes from roaming once more to the spot where Holly stood.

"Are you Chance Masters?" A pretty brunette with her hair pulled into pigtails grabbed his arm.

Frowning, Chance nodded. "How can I help you?"

"Not me, Holly. I'm Amanda, her best friend and part-time babysitter. I was there last night watching TV when you brought her home? Anyway, I'll explain all that later, or she can. Right now I need you to walk over to her and tell her it's time to go." She spoke fast, but he understood everything she said.

Chance frowned at the odd request. "Why would I do that?"

"Because that creepy guy won't leave her alone."

She grabbed his shirtsleeve and forcibly turned him around. There was Holly, a baby still in her arms. She was reaching out to take a kite from the man, who didn't appear to want to relinquish it.

"Got it?" the brunette asked from just behind him.

"Got it."

"Tell Holly I'll see her back at the house." She beat a path toward the main parking area.

As Chance stepped forward, Holly had apparently given up on retrieving the kite and was walking toward the parking lot at a swift pace, frustration and a hint of anger covering her face. The man she'd been talking to was trailing behind. Chance changed course, which put him directly in her path. She appeared shocked to see him there but immediately smiled in relief.

"You two look like you've had a good time."

"Gootine."

This one would be talking Holly's ear off in a matter of weeks.

"Pekite." The baby pointed to the kite in the man's hand.

"Yep." Chance nodded. "That's definitely one pink kite."

"Fye!" Emma pointed to the clouds.

"What brings you out to Kite Day?" Holly smiled up at him. He clearly read the silent message of "don't leave us" in her eyes.

Chance glanced at his watch. "Did you forget you asked me to pick you up at three?"

That brought a full grin. "Oh! I did! I totally forgot."

The man who'd been standing behind them stepped up next to Holly. He didn't look happy. He wore a Western hat, had a short beard, thin nose and narrow, glaring eyes. He was shorter than Chance but a good fifty pounds heavier, most of it around the waist.

"Oh, sorry," Holly said. "Blake, this is US Naval Commander Chance Masters. Chance, Blake, ah…Lufkin."

Chance offered his hand to the man. He seemed to consider his options before he accepted it, apparently deciding that to refuse in front of Holly would not be wise. As first impressions went, Chance didn't like the guy. Holly's friend had been right. Something about him felt off. Holly seemed determined to leave his company. Hell, Chance would help her with that in a heartbeat.

"Are you guys ready to go home?"

"Yes," she responded immediately. "It's been a long day."

"Why don't you let me take you home?" Blake asked, his hand rubbing her back with a familiarity that suggested it was something he did all the time. "We could run into town and grab an early dinner?"

"Uh, thanks," Holly said and moved away from his touch to stand next to Chance. "But actually I'm not hungry."

Holly was being way too polite. Chance slid his arm around her shoulders, giving her a kiss on the temple. "I'm parked right over here, sweetheart." Chance pointed in the opposite direction. "I'll take their kite off your hands."

When Chance grabbed the kite, the man didn't immediately release it. Chance didn't really care how he retrieved the baby's kite. The man could hand it to him from flat on his back, or save himself a whole lot of trouble. But after staring at Chance a few more seconds, he did the wise thing and let go, dropping his hand.

Holly wished Blake a good evening. He returned a stiff smile, clearly not happy Chance had interfered with whatever he had planned. Chance understood all too well. The man was a parasite, thinking Holly was alone and vulnerable, which only proved that the guy didn't know

Holly at all. She might be alone, but *vulnerable* wasn't in her vocabulary.

He opened the back door of his truck and set the kite on the seat. He didn't have a baby seat. It wasn't something he'd ever needed. Holly hopped up into the passenger side and set Emma on her lap, drawing the seat belt around both of them.

Chance got in behind the wheel and started the engine, still watching as the man walked off, finally disappearing amid the trees and parked cars.

"So spill," Chance said. "What's the deal with that guy?"

"I don't really know." She shrugged. "He moved here sometime last year. He came into the clinic for some flea and tick meds. The next thing I know he's showing up almost everywhere I go."

"He's asked you out?"

"Yeah. Like today. I've never accepted. The last time, I was pretty blunt. And I lied. I told him there was someone else in my life and I would not accept any invitations from him or anyone else." Holly took a deep breath. "I was afraid for a while I'd hurt his feelings and felt really bad about it, but two weeks later, here we go again. Small town. Guess it wasn't that hard to find out the truth. There is just something about him that makes me very uncomfortable."

"Has he ever threatened you?"

"No. Nothing like that. He's always polite. But…he's pushy. And he gets in my personal space." She shuddered. "I just wish he would go away. Go hit on somebody else."

Chance put the transmission in Drive. He would ensure Holly's wishes were met. No woman should have to deal with a stalker. He glanced at the baby in Holly's arms. "You haven't introduced me." He looked back at Holly. "Is she yours?"

That brought an immediate smile. "I thought you knew. This is Emma."

Obviously some things had definitely changed around here. Holly was a mother. And no one had thought it important enough to share that little tidbit of information?

Chance turned the truck toward the exit and the road that would take them back to the ranch.

"I'll send a ranch hand back for your truck, if that's okay. I'd prefer to make sure you both get home safely."

"Thank you, Chance."

He couldn't help but speculate about the father of the baby. Holly didn't wear a wedding ring, and although they hadn't had a chance to talk very much, surely she would not have come out to the barn and snuggled up next to him if she had a husband waiting at home.

A baby. Yet Holly still had that air of innocence. Obviously he was reading her wrong. Way wrong. Between her natural beauty and the fact she had a child, she couldn't be all that naive. Obviously there was a man in her life or had been at some point. These days, women didn't need a wedding ring on their finger to have a child. Some preferred it that way. He knew plenty of women, both in the military and not, who had one or more kids. Most said they neither wanted nor needed a man to complicate their life. He respected them even though he tended to be from the old school. Of the three Masters sons, he'd been the one closest to his mother and consequently had been raised with her principles. Old family values he'd never had reason to question. But in today's world, those ideas were outdated.

Chance's life didn't make it easy to have a permanent girlfriend or a wife, although some in his platoon were married and, at least on the outside, appeared to make it work. He liked his life the way it was. He was responsible only to himself and during a mission, the safety of his team. Kids were not something he wanted to be around, let alone be responsible for. Generally a baby was not something that put a smile on his face. They were a constant reminder of just how narrow the line between life and death was. They made him see the hopelessness of ever having peace in this world. He needed to stay away from Holly anyway, out of respect. A baby might just be the ticket to ensure he kept his distance.

Five

Sunday morning Holly finished feeding Emma her breakfast of oatmeal and juice, then set her down on a pallet to play with her five-note legless piano, her favorite toy.

"Aren't you late for your date?" Amanda asked as she refilled her coffee cup. "It's after eight o'clock."

"I told you, Amanda, it isn't a date. And we really didn't set a time." Holly stepped into the bathroom and began braiding her hair. "Are you sure you're willing to watch Emma on a Sunday?"

"Absolutely. As hard as you work, you deserve

to enjoy a day off now and then. Anyway *Slanders Ridge* is coming on at two. That's about when Emma takes her nap. I'll just let her doze on the couch with me. We'll be fine. Go. Enjoy your day. With that hunk, how could you not?"

Holly took in a deep breath and sighed. She was separated from Emma too much during a normal workweek. She hated missing a day with her on a weekend. The guilt weighed heavily. But this was only one day. Not even an entire day. And how often did she get an opportunity to go riding with Chance? She would make it up to Emma. Definitely.

She hadn't made it out the door when her cell went off. Chance.

"Good morning."

"Good morning to you. Are you ready for that ride?"

"Definitely."

"I'll see you at the barn."

"On my way."

With a hug for Amanda and a kiss for Emma, Holly slipped on her boots, pulled the jean pant legs down over the boot tops and she was ready. "I'll see you later."

"Be careful. Have fun."

The increased volume of the television drowned out anything else that might have been said.

Stepping into the barn, she saw no sign of Chance. She walked down the main aisle to the big gray gelding that nickered when he saw her. She grabbed the halter that hung on the stall door, slipped it on and led him to the grooming area next to the tack room.

"Good morning," Chance said as he walked inside the barn a few minutes later. His deep voice sounded husky, as though he'd just awakened. His short dark hair was in disarray. He was wearing jeans and a blue sleeveless shirt, unbuttoned and hanging from his broad shoulders. The sculptured muscles of his chest and abs were amazing.

"Good morning to you."

Holding his coffee cup in one hand, Chance sidled toward her, approaching the gray horse cautiously as if he was afraid his presence would startle it.

"I didn't know we had any thoroughbreds."

"I don't think you do. This is Sinbad and he's mine. He's actually a thoroughbred-Arabian mix. Cole lets me keep him here in exchange for being on call for the ranch but I pay for his food."

Chance ran his hand over the velvety neck. "He's nice."

Holly smiled. "Thanks."

Chance nodded his head in approval. "Well, I guess I need to catch up."

Stretching his arms, he walked to the center aisle, scanning the horses. He selected a big bay quarter horse that nickered to him as he passed, a good indication he was ready to leave his stall for a while. With the efficiency gained over a lifetime, Chance quickly brushed down then saddled the gelding.

"Do you need any help?" he asked, returning to Holly, leading the bay behind him.

"No, thanks. I've got it." She threw a red plaid saddle blanket onto Sinbad's back, then followed with a Western saddle. She tightened the girth, switched from a halter to a bridle and was ready to go.

Holly couldn't help but notice that Chance seemed to hesitate before climbing into the saddle. She'd forgotten he'd been wounded.

"Chance, if you're still recovering, we don't have to do this. Don't do anything that might set your recovery back."

Absently he rubbed his left arm. He obviously didn't want to talk about it and he was right. Talking wouldn't make it heal any faster and the last thing he needed was pity. Still…

"You might tear cartilage or undo the healing. It isn't worth the risk."

He looked out over the vast pastureland. "Yeah, it is."

The gelding was spirited and anxious to get started, but had been well trained, as had his rider. The horse stood in place while Chance jumped up, slid his left boot in the stirrup and threw his right leg over the saddle. He looked back at Holly. "We're good. Let's go."

Gathering the reins, he directed the bay toward the main gate that led to the bulk of the ranch land. Holly was happy to follow. They headed west, toward the river. Neither seemed inclined to talk. It was a day to relax and enjoy and Chance seemed intent on fully taking advantage of being here. Holly sensed he needed the quiet so she rode along next to him without attempting conversation.

They rode for miles. Spring rain had made the rolling pastures a deep, rich green. Chance appeared to visibly relax as they rode farther into the trees that dotted the land. Eventually they topped a rise and saw the river below. She could hear the sound of rushing water over the rock bed.

"Want to stop for a while?" She hoped he wouldn't think she was mothering him, even if she was.

"Yeah," he replied. "We can do that. I remember…there. On that gray boulder. You and Jason and I would sit and talk. Remember?"

"Yes. About girls." She rolled her eyes but was pleased he remembered. A lot of life had been discussed on that boulder. Past worries laid to rest; future dreams shared. Sometimes she'd been allowed to go along.

"How old were you back then?"

She thought for a moment. "I think around nine, maybe ten. You and Jason were still in high school. Aunt Ida used to make Jason take me with him. He would get so mad." Holly had to smile at the memory. Gosh, how she missed Jason. Aunt Ida, too.

Dismounting, they tethered the horses and climbed onto the large rock that jutted out over the water. The shade of the oak and cottonwood trees was cool on her back. The sound of the rushing water was always melodic and relaxing. Soon Chance sat down next to her.

"Remember when we all used to come here thinking we could catch fish for supper?"

He chuckled. "Yes. And if memory serves, we did catch some once. They weren't as big as your hand but you insisted on taking them home anyway."

"Your chef looked at that stringer as though he was being asked to panfry a snake."

"I know. But the guy tried. Then after one bite you determined they were uneatable." Chance laughed. "Double whammy. Poor man."

"Didn't he quit not long after that?"

"Yeah, he did."

Holly lay back on the rock. The radiant warmth felt good.

Chance chuckled. "Do you still have the old shoe?" he asked, referring to a centuries-old high-top shoe they'd found inside the remnants of an old cabin.

"Yep. It's wrapped in tissue and inside a zip-lock bag. It seems a shame to keep it tucked away. I mean, it would be nice to display it some-where, but I'm so afraid something might happen to it. I wish we could have found the other one."

"So do I. That was definitely one of our bet-ter finds."

"Yes. That and the compass." Holly glanced over at Chance. "Do you still have it?"

"Yeah. And Jason brought the razor and the musket balls over to the house before he left for college. It's hard to believe part of the Civil War took place in our own pasture. I wonder if the old cabin on the rise is still standing."

"I doubt it. But maybe we can check it out be-fore you...while you're here."

There was a lull in the conversation. Then...

"How old is your baby?"

She rolled toward him, a smile pulling at the corners of her mouth. "Fourteen months," she answered without any hesitation.

Chance lay on the boulder, one boot crossed over his raised knee, his hands threaded under his head, his eyes closed as he doubtlessly listened to the peacefulness around him.

"She's Jason's daughter. You do know that, right?"

He looked over at her. "No. I didn't have any idea."

"His wife died giving birth a few months after Jason was killed. Carolyn didn't have any family so I brought Emma home. When I look at her I see a little bit of Jason. But Emma is a person in her own right. She's so smart she's a handful. You work to keep up with that one."

Chance rolled toward her, his head propped on his hand. She looked into those smoky-blue eyes and wanted to drown in them. She saw his pupils widen as he gazed at her with serious intent.

She wanted to kiss him. She wanted to know how he tasted, how his hot breath would feel on her skin, how his big hands would feel when they touched her. He was so sexy, so handsome. Most of all, he was Chance. He'd saved her from school bullies, taught her to ride a bicycle, then bandaged her knee when she took a tumble. She'd loved him when he'd signed up and joined the navy and had never stopped thinking of him in the twelve long years he'd been gone. He wasn't the same man she'd known then. Wherever he'd been, whatever he'd been doing had changed him from the happy-go-lucky cowboy, defying his billionaire status, into a hardened warrior. Clearly he was used to being in command.

"I'm surprised you're not married." she said, feeling a bit awkward for some reason.

"What I do doesn't leave a lot of room for serious relationships. Here one day, gone the next, and no way of knowing when I'll be back. Sometimes it's a week. Sometimes nine months or longer."

"I can see how that would be tough," she agreed. "A woman would have to be strong and completely head over heels in love to deal with that."

"Yeah. And have the trust and patience of a saint. And they are rare. Some of the guys in my platoon are married. But it's hard on the relationship. Eventually he begins to question if she's faithful, and if that concern takes root and stays on his mind it can get him killed. It's equally hard on the woman for obvious reasons. One guy in my unit, Ray Shields, has three kids. He never got to be there for the birth of any of them."

"But some do make it work."

"Yeah. Some do."

"Why did you never come back here before now? You loved the ranch so much."

He was quiet for so long she wasn't sure he would answer.

"Too many memories. And most of them were not so great. I guess you knew my father and I didn't get along. I think the entire county knew. Or maybe you were too young to pick up on it. But there was a lot of resentment. On both sides. I blamed him for the death of my mother. Still do. He blamed me for a hell of a lot, as well." He paused, as though transported deep into his past. "It seemed like the wisest move to take my leaves somewhere else."

After a long silence, Chance sat up and scanned the horizon. "It looks like rain is coming our way. Are you ready to head back?"

"I guess. If you are."

She wanted to ask him so much more about his mother. Holly had very little recollection of her. But now wasn't the time. She sat up next to him and their gazes met and held. How she wanted to kiss him. Right here. Right now. Right or wrong. She couldn't think of a better place for something she'd waited for for a lifetime. Moving closer to his muscled body, her focus dropped to his mouth. Absently, she moistened her lips.

"Holly." He shook his head.

"What?"

"This is not a good idea." His voice was rough, as though he was holding himself back.

"I don't know what you're talking about." But her focus remained on his lips that had haunted her for over a decade, now a mere breath away.

"Yeah. You do." But despite his hesitation, he reached up and smoothed some strands of her hair back from her face. He caught the back of her hair in his fist, gently pulling her toward him. In what seemed like slow motion, she watched as his face came closer. His lips parted, showing a glimpse of strong white teeth. Then his mouth touched hers, gently at first, his lips moving over hers tentatively, as though he was giving her every opportunity to change her mind. He drew back, making her heart cry out. He watched her, carefully, intently, as though he had to be sure this was what she wanted.

"It's just a kiss," she whispered. She could hear the pleading in her own voice.

"Don't bullshit me," Chance said. "We both know it's a hell of a lot more than that."

She raised her hand and touched his face, letting her fingers trail over his deep jaw, feeling the stubble, while her eyes remained fixed on his handsome face. With a last glance, the lure of his lips could no longer be denied. She tilted her head and swayed toward him. Chance pulled her the rest of the way. Strong yet supple, with his tongue he moistened her as though preparing her for something more to come. Then the gentleness was gone as he took her mouth fully and completely. His tongue pushed inside and she was lost. A shiver ran through her at the speed of his immediate possession.

Holly savored the feel and taste of him. Her arms came around his neck, holding him to her. She heard him inhale a deep breath, felt the grip on the back of her hair tighten in his fist. He tasted of raw, hungry male, his mouth and tongue so hot, so demanding, it threatened to overwhelm her senses. Heat surged through her veins like liquid lava, pooling at the apex of her legs.

She felt the warm sensation of the rock against her back and absently realized she was lying prone with Chance's hard body covering hers. He was ravenous. His mouth moved rapidly over hers, taking her over and over, pushing his tongue in deep time after time. She heard him emit a growl, long and low, and her body responded. She wanted more. She needed more as his mouth continued to ravish hers, over and over, entering the deep recesses of her mouth, seeking the hidden depths, encouraging her to do the same.

His big hand cupped her breast, kneading her almost to the point of pain but never crossing the line, making her sensitive flesh swell under his touch. She arched her back, wanting to cry out at the sheer pleasure. She couldn't get close enough, couldn't open to him wide enough, take him deep enough.

As if he could read her mind, he made a simple adjustment and Holly felt his erection pressed hard against her. She couldn't hold back the moan, the last sound she heard before reality disappeared and left her floating in Chance's arms. Something seized her deep inside. It was a feeling that burned her like an invisible ray of the sun, heating her skin, surging through her body like a forest fire out of control. It made her forget to breathe, caused her heart to speed up and her mouth to go dry. The sheer intensity of it was indescribable. Her body ached as though she was experiencing withdrawals. She had never felt such a strong physical attraction to anyone before in her life.

Suddenly Chance raised his head, separating their hungry lips, breathing hard. Their gazes locked for endless seconds before Chance rolled away, mumbling some not-so-nice words under his breath. Still, his nearness made her intensely aware of his rock-hard masculinity, the sheer density and power of his body. The sudden stillness poured over her like the cold waters of the stream. Holly wanted to scream at him, beg him to release the building frustration and make it stop. She wanted him to free the overwhelming desire rising inside her, ease the terrible throbbing need to be loved by him.

The world came sliding back and try as she might, she couldn't stop it. The sound of the running water slowly returned. Birds called in the trees. The branches above them swayed in the gentle breeze, the shadows moving over the two people below like soft caresses.

Holly realized she was lying on her back on the huge rock, her blouse unbuttoned, her body seizing up and needing more. She squeezed her legs together, trying to ease the need, and rolled onto one shoulder to watch as Chance wrestled with what had happened.

"Don't you dare even think about apologizing." He turned his head to look into her face. Remorse showed clearly in every feature, confirming that was exactly what he was thinking.

"Holly—"

"No. Not one word. Not one syllable. Please don't ruin it. I'm just sorry you stopped."

"Don't say that." His voice was incredibly deep and gravelly with a hint of desperation.

"Why not? It's the truth."

Chance shook his head, then rubbed the back of his neck and mumbled something she couldn't understand.

"Don't grumble," she said as she began buttoning her blouse.

Chance looked over at her as though there was something he needed to say. A whole bunch of things. Instead, he straightened his spine, ran one weary hand over his face and groaned.

The ride back was quiet, but not strained. Holly let Sin go at his own pace. She kept her head turned away so Chance didn't see the smile that refused to leave her face as she relived their embrace. That had definitely been worth waiting for. But it wasn't just the kiss or the passion that flared between them. Chance had been right when he'd said there was a lot more to it. Their embrace had been life changing. It had affirmed that childhood was over. Thinking of him as merely a friend was history.

Part of her was thrilled that Chance was attracted to her. The other part reminded her that whatever they shared while he was here would soon be just another memory. And she'd be well advised to remember that.

Six

The sprawling city of Dallas spread out beneath them as the chopper headed toward a landing pad located somewhere in the muddle below. It was a far different sight from flying over the cities in Afghanistan and Iraq. Sitting next to Cole, Chance was content to gaze out the window and let the pilot do his thing. No reason to try to talk over the roar of the engine. They both knew where they were headed and why. It wasn't enough for Wade to tell him about the corporation and the plans for future development—he wanted to show him. Chance had refrained from telling him he didn't succumb to arm-twisting and wasn't about to start now.

Cole pointed to a skyscraper on Chance's right. Constructed of steel and smoked glass, it gave the impression of wealth, power and sophistication. Soon the helipad came into view and the pilot set down in a near-perfect maneuver on top of the building. A short trip to the elevator and then they were walking down a richly carpeted hallway to Wade's office.

Chance expected to greet only Wade, but the sprawling office and reception area was filled with people. Applause broke out as soon as he walked through the door. Chance understood they were heralding one of their soldiers' return home from the battlefield, but he could have done without the attention. He shook hands and received gentle pats on the back as he made his way to where his eldest brother stood as the employees who'd welcomed him filed out the door.

When they all had departed, Wade lost no time getting down to business. Literally. For the next five hours Chance was given a thorough glimpse into Masters Corporation, Ltd. It was impressive.

Wade had done an excellent job and Chance lost no time telling him so. The plans for future expansion in key areas were brilliant. Wade was made for this and he handled it beautifully. Cole proudly gave Chance a bird's-eye view of the books: where they had been, where they were now and where they expected to be in the next two years.

"Where are the figures on the ranch?"

He caught a quick glance pass from Cole to Wade. Suddenly the feeling of camaraderie in the room shifted to one of nervous tension. It was the same sensation Chance felt on missions when they had been given wrong intel and rather than a simple reconnaissance his team found themselves in the middle of an all-out skirmish. There was always a moment of realization that they'd been set up just before shit hit the fan and bullets started to fly, not unlike what he was feeling right now. The hair on the back of his neck stood at attention. Chance stepped back from the conference table and waited.

"The fact is," Cole said, meeting Chance's eyes, "the ranch is not profitable. It hasn't been for the past five or six years. Beef prices fluctuate but the cost to maintain it steadily goes up."

"There is a lot more to it than that. Have you taken an in-depth look at the figures?"

"Yes. And no."

"What the hell does that mean?"

"It means we've decided to get out of the cattle business. There is a lot more money to be made in other areas of the corporation. Frankly, we are not ranchers. We've tried several times to bring in someone to manage a turnaround. Nothing they tried worked. It's just not worth the money and time to try to fix whatever might be wrong—if there is a fix—when that time could be better spent working on financially sound investment opportunities."

"The ranch was Mom's dream."

Wade nodded. "Yes, it was. But she's gone. And times have changed. The land itself is worth more divided into parcels and sold for development than it is as a feeding trough for cattle. Plus, the entire west end of the property runs parallel to the rail system, which triples its worth."

Chance clenched his jaw, determined to keep

that sickening twist in his gut from spilling out in a completely different form, all directed at his brothers. He clenched his fists as fury battled desperation. In all the covert missions, he'd never felt such a strong sense of pending disaster. There was always a plan B. There was always hope. But this was a dagger right to the heart. And he had only himself to blame. He was the one who'd chosen to walk away, leaving Wade and Cole to handle it all. As it stood, he had no right to say anything. He'd long ago made choices, and those choices took him out of the game. But that didn't stop the bile from rising in his throat.

From the home office, they were driven to the original Masters mansion in North Dallas, where dinner would be served and they would spend the night. Their grandfather had built the original structure back in the 1940s. Their father had doubled its size, and the entire building had been updated just before he died. Complete with turrets, it had always reminded Chance of something out of the Middle Ages. This was where Wade and Cole had lived the first few years of their life and, when business brought them to Dallas, this was home. Their mother had not been raised in a city and longed for the wide-open spaces, so to appease her, the gigantic log-and-stone house at the ranch had been built. That was the only home Chance could remember.

While Wade and Cole kept up a lively conversation between courses, Chance's mind wavered between the loss of the ranch and Holly. Somehow he saw both in the same light. In a matter of weeks, he would lose them both. He would head back to his world, and life would continue as it had for the past twelve years. He couldn't help but surmise what would happen to her business if Wade sold the land. Could a veterinarian clinic survive amidst the housing developments and commercial ventures? He supposed it could happen. Maybe she would be better off. Maybe Cole would help her relocate. Whatever happened, Holly would survive. She was a fighter. Always had been.

Chance shouldn't have kissed her. He'd promised himself he wouldn't touch her. But damn. He was glad he had even if it was wrong. She'd felt amazing in his arms. Her skin was velvety soft and smooth. She'd melted against him until it felt as if the two had merged into one. He'd never felt that close to any woman, even during sex. The silky sweetness of her mouth had been almost more than he could handle without taking her fully. And he'd wanted to. The way she'd opened to him, offering more… Her soft moans telling him of her need. Holding himself back had taken more strength and determination than a lot of the missions he faced as a SEAL.

She had a baby. A baby not a lot older than the one he'd let die. He'd been in plenty of situations he would label uncomfortable. Being around her baby was another one. He couldn't tell Holly he no longer wanted to be around her because she had a kid. And he wanted to see her again. Whether it was right or wrong, whatever this thing was between them had changed from childhood friendship to adult desire, and it gripped him hard and heavy. He'd felt the very real, very hot flames of it when he'd kissed her. When she'd responded.

His brothers' laughter brought him back to the present.

"That sound okay with you, Chance?"

"I'm sorry?"

Wade had that stupid knowing smile on his face again. "I was saying a welcome-home celebration was needed. It'll give you the opportunity to meet some of the executive staff here in Dallas. We have some really good people and they've all been waiting to meet you. I think once you have a chance to talk with them, get to know them and feel comfortable, this whole corporation thing won't seem so alien to you."

Chance sat up in his chair. The last thing he wanted to do was become a G.I. Joe puppet on Wade's center stage. Clearly this was another attempt by his brothers to bring him on board at the company, and after their earlier revelation about the ranch, he wanted nothing more than to tell them both to stick it. "And who else will be there?"

"Excuse me?"

"Other than your employees?"

Wade dropped the linen napkin on the table.

"There might be some representatives from companies we do business with."

"You see me as a salable, item and you're not going to let the opportunity pass to draw interest to your latest project by introducing them to a SEAL. And the fact that it's your own brother makes it more palatable. You never were one to give up an opportunity to grab for the brass ring. Just like Dad."

Wade shrugged. "I'm not saying you're right, but even if you are? So what?"

Chance looked at Cole, who had silently observed the exchange. "You want explain it to him?"

"Cole doesn't have to explain anything to me," Wade barked, his voice edged with aggravation and long-practiced intimidation.

Yeah. Good luck with that.

"I get that you want no part of this company, Chance. I think I can change your mind but you've got to give me an opportunity. What can it possibly hurt for you to put a little effort forward and meet some people? People who care a lot about you."

"I don't even know them. You said that yourself."

This conversation had no end. He and his brother could keep arguing until the next full moon. No, it couldn't hurt for Chance to agree to attend this fiasco, but at the same time, it wouldn't hurt for Wade to let it go.

Chance blew out a breath. "It seems ridiculous to me when I have no plans to stay. I'll do it. But one evening is it. After that, no more."

"Done," Wade confirmed.

"If you gentlemen will excuse me, I think I'll say good-night. I've had about all the happy news I can stomach for one evening." Chance stood and looked around at where he'd been sitting. They'd used three chairs out of the forty that surrounded the elaborate table, the rich mahogany gleaming under the glow of three chandeliers. "Why don't you put some effort toward getting a smaller table? Eventually somebody's going to think there are a lot of guests who didn't show up for dinner. Not good for the image." He pursed his lips at the humor apparently only he could see. "Good night."

As Chance's long strides carried him down the hall to the elevator, he heard his brothers discussing what they had asked him to do. Cole wanted the party held here, in the center of Dallas, which would be easier on everybody. Except for the star attraction, aka the bait. In two days he had an appointment with the civilian doctor. Depending on his findings, Chance would be one step closer to getting back to his team.

The next morning, not willing to subject himself to the possibility of any belated plans Wade may have thought of overnight, he asked the chauffeur to take him to the heliport. Wade and Cole had meetings scheduled in Dallas over the next two days, so there was really no reason to stick around just to say goodbye. They knew where to reach him if need be, plus there was an abundance of choppers if anyone needed to make a fast trip back to the ranch or anywhere else.

Soon Chance was behind the controls, the rotors gaining speed as he lifted off, heading the chopper north. This was a toy compared with what he'd been trained to fly, but it handled well enough. When the sprawling ranch came into view, only then did he begin to relax.

He had just shut down the engine of the Bell 407GX and stepped away from the chopper when his cell began to ring. It was Holly.

"Hey, Holly."

"How was your visit to Dallas?"

"Oh, wonderful." He could hear the heavy sarcasm in his own voice. There were dogs barking in the background on her end so he didn't hear her reply.

"Come to dinner. Tonight at seven. It's meat loaf night."

"Meat loaf, huh? How can I pass that up?"

She giggled. "Gotta go. See ya then."

He couldn't help but notice his steps were lighter than they'd been before she called. But as he reached the flagstone area around the pool, he remembered the baby who would no doubt be there tonight. How was he going to spend time in the presence of...what was her name? *Emma?* How could he carry on as though it was nothing? Every time he looked at Holly's baby he saw the baby girl in Iraq. She'd been sitting on the ground innocently playing with a doll. Chance had heard the missile seconds before he saw the exhaust as it lined up trajectory to the target: a building directly behind where the child sat.

He'd hauled ass toward the baby, muscles straining as he pushed himself past his physical limits, determined to get there in time. The explosion had blown him back some thirty feet. He'd lost hearing in one ear for almost a month, and they'd pulled shrapnel from his head and shoulders, requiring several days in the infirmary. And when the dust settled, there was nothing of the baby that remained. Just one foot of the little doll. All he could do was lie in that hospital bed and relive the incident over and over. Three seconds. If he'd had three seconds more, he might have saved her.

It was a child Emma's age who brought on the nightmares. Of all the things he'd witnessed during his time in the service, that had been the worst. It had brought the reality of just how innocent and fragile a little life was screaming to the surface. After that experience, he'd stayed well away from members of his platoon who incessantly talked about their families. He didn't blame them. Not at all. But it was nothing he would ever be a part of, and he found reasons to leave the room before new baby pictures made the rounds. He was happy for Holly. She seemed to really love Emma and no doubt was a great mom. But it was none of his business and it needed to stay that way.

Chance ran a hand over his face. He should listen to his own common sense. This wasn't Iraq. There were no guided missiles. Holly's baby was fine. He would be there an hour tops. He could do an hour. He wanted to see Holly again. If that's the only way he could do it, he would get through it somehow.

"Come in!" Holly called upon hearing the knock on the door. Seeing Chance step into the room, she left the potatoes frying in the pan and hurried over to give him a welcome hug.

"Smells good," he said and hugged her back.

"I hope you like it. It's my granny's recipe." She hurried back to the stove. "There's cold beer in the fridge and dinner is almost ready."

This was the first time she'd ever cooked for Chance. She'd debated for two days what to fix. She wanted it to be something he couldn't get anywhere else. That ruled out steak and baked potatoes. With her limited culinary skills, she'd settled on her Granny's secret meat loaf recipe, homemade French fries, green beans from Miss Annie's garden and cold beer or mint tea. Holly would have never been able to pick out or afford a good wine anyway.

Placing the food on the table, she told him to take a seat before hurrying from the room to get Emma. Chance's body language changed when she carried the baby into the dining room. He appeared to withdraw. She had to wonder what that was about. Setting the high chair at the table between them, she seated Emma, then fixed her plate: noodles, some of the fries, green beans and applesauce. Finally, Holly sat down in the vacant chair across from Chance.

"Please, help yourself."

Without uttering a word, Chance cut a sizable portion of the meat loaf and helped himself to the fries, green beans and a hot roll. He periodically glanced at Emma almost as though she made him nervous. Odd. He'd seemed fine with her at the Kite Festival at the park. Maybe he'd just had a bad day.

With Emma, it was sink or swim. She would either like you or she wouldn't. It was her decision. If she took to Chance, he'd made a friend for life. Holly sat back, content to see what Emma would do.

It didn't take long.

The baby was fascinated with the big man. She chewed a noodle and watched him fork a bite of meat into his mouth.

"This is great, Holly." He glanced at Emma, who still sat staring at the new person in their house.

"Bea." She pointed to the green beans on his plate. When Chance didn't move she apparently thought he didn't understand her command. She leaned over toward Chance, her hand almost touching his plate. "Bea."

"Right. Bean."

But he didn't put any beans on his fork. He didn't pick one up. He didn't put any in his mouth. And Emma became more determined, staring as if trying to figure out why this person sitting at the table wasn't eating his food.

Chance speared some fries. That seemed to appease her somewhat. She looked at her own plate and picked up a fry. As she chewed, she continued to stare at Chance. Holly had to wonder if Chance felt like a specimen under a microscope. It was then she noticed the beads of perspiration on his forehead. She stood from the table and walked to the thermostat on the wall, cranking it down a few degrees. When she returned to the table, Chance was wiping his face.

"Are you okay?"

"Yeah. Fine. This is really good."

"So seriously, how'd it go in Dallas with your brothers?"

He shrugged. "Pretty much the way I expected."

She saw the muscles in his jaw working overtime. He took a deep breath as though trying to gain control. Something unexpected had happened. Something he clearly didn't want to talk about. She wouldn't push him to tell her.

If he wanted her to know, he would when he was ready.

"Fy." Emma held out a French fry to Chance.

"Emma, here." Holly put some applesauce in a spoon and held it to Emma's mouth. "Take some applesauce. Mmm. Good."

The baby took the bite, never taking her eyes off Chance. Holly sat mesmerized as Emma grabbed a noodle in her chubby hand and held it out to Chance. The baby leaned far out of her high chair in an attempt to feed Chance the noodle. Holly would swear the color drained from his face.

"She won't give up until she sees you eating a green bean or a noodle. Those are her favorites." Holly smiled in apology. "She's like that. She tends to want to take care of people she likes."

Chance nodded his head and speared a bean. "She doesn't know me."

"She knows enough." Once Chance ate some of the green beans, Emma sat back in her chair, content. "Remember you telling me about that sixth sense you rely on? I'd have to say knowing which people she likes and doesn't is something like that. I've seen her scream bloody murder if a person she doesn't like tries to pick her up, even if it's a grandmotherly type and innocent as can be. You've just witnessed what happens when the vibes are right."

Chance cut a glance back at the baby. She sat quietly, watching him while she chewed on her bean. He picked up a French fry, broke it in two and gave her half. They both chewed their potato.

As the meal went on, Chance seemed to relax. A little. They shared green beans and more potatoes until finally Emma was full and wanted down to play.

"So where is your roommate this evening?"

"Roommate? Oh, you mean Amanda. She went home. Said she had errands to do. I think she had a date. She'll be back eventually. She gets lonely sitting in her apartment by herself. She's in between jobs right now."

"What does she do?"

"RN. Surgical nurse."

"You've known her a while?"

"Yeah. We've been friends since grade school.

Her dad is the pharmacist at City Drug. You might know him. Doug Stiller?"

"Yeah. Yeah I remember him." Chance wiped his hands on the napkin. "He was always very understanding when a guy's hormones began to kick it. But you didn't walk away with a foil packet in your back pocket without a speech about being responsible." He glanced at Holly and smiled. The glimmer was back in his eyes. "I tended to listen."

Emma banged her spoon on her tray and kicked her feet. "Out," she demanded loudly. Holly reached for Emma and knocked over a glass of lemonade. The liquid spilled onto Chance's half-eaten dinner.

"Oh! I'm sorry. Here, let me get another plate and some—"

"Don't worry about it, Holly. It was all delicious but I'm full."

"Boo-boo," Emma proclaimed.

"Yes. Boo-boo," Holly agreed, still mopping at the spill with whatever napkin she could find.

"It was really good, Holly. I'm sorry to eat and

run, but there are some things I need to do before tomorrow."

He stood from the table, careful of the baby, and headed to the back door.

Why did she suddenly feel like a waitress in a really bad restaurant?

"Sure. Maybe we can do it again sometime." She followed him to the door.

"Yeah. That'd be nice."

He pulled open the outside door and hesitated. She heard him mutter to himself before turning around and catching her face in his hands. He absorbed her lips, kissing her deeply, then took one last glance at Emma. "Good night."

And just like that he was gone. Holly turned to look at Emma, who sat contentedly on the floor, playing with a toy. Something had totally unnerved Chance. She had no clue what. Surely not Emma? Yet that was what appeared to be the problem. She began gathering the dirty dishes. She knew some men didn't like to be around children. Apparently Chance was one of them. One more reason for Holly to keep her distance.

For more than half of her life she'd daydreamed

about Chance. Of the home they would have, the family... The reality was very different and it was a hard pill to swallow. Knowing he would soon leave again, plus seeing his reaction to Emma pretty much said it all. There would never be a future for them. And the sooner she accepted it the better off she would be.

"Commander Masters?" Chance stood as the doctor held out a hand. "I'm Dr. Lopez. Good to meet you, sir. Please come in."

Chance followed the doctor into the small examination room.

"Your doctor at the VA forwarded a summary of your injuries. Tell me about them. How do *you* think you're doing?"

It was an intensive hour. This doctor, while not military, knew his stuff. After Chance explained how he felt physically and emotionally, the doctor examined him head to foot.

"Do you have full range of motion in your left shoulder?"

"Pretty much." He rubbed the site of the bullet's entry on his chest. "I still have minor pain around the site itself, but everything else feels normal. It's my knee I'm worried about."

The doctor nodded. "Hop on the table and let's have a look."

When the exam was finished, Chance went through a battery of tests including X-rays and an MRI on both his chest wound and his knee. Finally back in his office, the good doctor explained that the preliminary results looked good.

"It will take forty-eight hours to get all of the results back but I don't anticipate seeing any problems. Are you taking any physical therapy?"

"No."

"You might want to consider it. I would suggest you start out slow. Don't push your knee too hard at first. If you have access to a pool, that would be an excellent way to work the knee without an extraordinary amount of pressure."

The doctor leaned against the counter, looking at his file. "Are you going to return to active duty?"

"That's the plan."

The doctor tore a slip of paper from his prescription pad and handed it to Chance. It had a name, address and phone number. "Physical therapist. He's good. Call and set up a few sessions. I'll call you if there is anything that concerns me when the last of your tests come in."

While it was good to hear some positives, this doctor didn't know the specifics of Chance's job. Therefore he would have no way of knowing if Chance could return to doing it. It was damn hard to stay positive when it was your life on the line and your future was ultimately in the hands of the Naval Medical Evaluation Board.

Seven

"Let's start him out slow today," Mark Johansen called to Holly, who was seated atop her gray gelding, Sinbad. "Ease him into a slow canter, keeping to the outside of the cross rails."

Holly did as she was instructed. She loved riding Sin and he seemed equally happy to give her the ride. He was an amazing animal. He carried her smoothly twice around the large arena, never once slowing or breaking stride.

"Now," Mark called from the center of the ring, "when you get to the opposite end, gather him, take a half halt into a figure eight and ask him to change his gait. Then reverse when you reach the other end. We need him to feel like that's a normal motion."

Holly took Sin around again then gathered the reins, gave the cue, and within a few strides Sin switched from leading with his right front foot to his left.

"Try that again. He needs to respond more quickly. Take him around a few more times. Keep in a figure eight. He should start to feel it as part of his natural stride, changing without you asking him to do it depending on the direction."

Holly gave a nod and followed Mark's instructions. The fourth time, Sin switched his lead perfectly. Holly finished the round, patting Sin on the neck, then directed him toward the inside of the arena for the jumps.

The first cavalletti was a cross rail: two poles that crossed one another with a straight beam over the top. At four feet in height, it was a piece of cake for Sinbad. Holly lined him up for the jump, gathered the reins and gave the cue. With graceful ease, the powerful gelding sailed over the jump as though he was floating on air. Her body automatically swung forward as Sin left the ground. The horse's natural motion lifted her rear out of the saddle, then her weight sank back into the stirrups as they landed. She continued around the small course, Sin taking each jump as perfectly as the first.

Twice more through the maze and Mark waved her over. "Okay. He did great on the jumps but he still needs some work on dressage."

She glanced over toward the indoor bleachers. Near the front entrance Emma contentedly played with her own little plastic horses and cows inside the playpen. The indoor arena was actually a little larger than the one outside. It allowed for storage of the jumps and ensured Emma a near-perfect temperature year-round. Out of the corner of her eye she caught movement. Chance was leaning against the railing. How long had he been there?

"Chance. Come over and meet Mark."

"Mark, this is Chance Masters. He is one of the owners of this ranch."

"Mark Johansen. Nice to meet you." The men

shook hands. "You have an incredible spread here."

"Thanks."

Holly turned to Chance. "Mark was once a contender for the US Olympic team. He and his wife moved here last year and he's been kind enough to give me some dressage and show-jumping lessons," Holly said. "What's it been? Six months?"

"About that," Mark replied. "She's doing great."

Chance nodded. "Yeah. I saw. Lots of *passion* in that ring. It would undoubtedly have me on my back begging for mercy in about eight seconds." His deep blue eyes sparkled with dark humor.

Holly knew he was referring to their night in the barn when she told him about her new fervor. "Yep. It tends to make a girl wild-child crazy. Controlling all that power." She couldn't help but grin as Chance put two and two together.

"I should have known you were talking about a horse." He shook his head.

"Why, Commander, what else could it have been?" she asked, a grin edging her lips, a look of pure innocence on her face.

Chance didn't reply to her challenge but his eyes told her in no uncertain terms that payback would be hell.

"I'm out of here," Mark said. "Mary Ann, my wife, has a list of to-dos. It was nice to meet you, Chance," he said and headed for his truck.

"I need to talk to you. Would you mind stopping by the house when you're finished?" Chance asked Holly when they were alone.

She shrugged. "Sure. Let me put Sin back in his stall and I'll be there."

"Take your time," he said before turning and disappearing around the corner of the barn.

After Sinbad was showered down, brushed out and returned to his stall with some apple slices in his feeding trough, she picked up Emma and headed for the big house.

Holly rarely came here. She'd been inside once or twice as a child, gotten lost and, after a kindly housekeeper showed the way back outside, she'd never tried again. Chance was rarely in the house. Their time together was always spent in or around the barn.

She let herself through the back gate that

opened into the courtyard. From here she had a view of miles and miles of rolling hills blanketed by well-fertilized grass, so green it almost didn't look real. She passed the waterfall at one end of the large lagoon-style swimming pool, and Emma laughed when a few drops of cold water hit her in the face. She squealed and worked her feet in an attempt to get down. Holly held firm. Emma would be in that pool in a heartbeat and all the beautiful tropical plants she could reach along the way would meet their demise. Emma had a deep love for all things nature, especially the flowers. But she wanted to pick them all. Holly hadn't as yet convinced her they could be enjoyed just as much on the bush outside. She passed through the outdoor kitchen and under the large pergola to the back entrance.

She rang the bell, letting Chance know she was there. She thought she heard a voice, so she opened the door. "Hello?"

Chance appeared on the catwalk above with a towel wrapped around his waist. "Come on in. I had to take a quick shower. Be down in a minute."

"Okay." She stepped inside and looked around. Someone had gone to great lengths to downplay the family's wealth in the decor, but while she liked the Western theme, it failed to conceal the pure luxury around her. With a stone fireplace on the wall to the left large enough to roast an entire cow, this single room was larger than her entire house. The furnishings were leather, the kind that a person could just sink down into. Curious, she peeked around the corner just beyond the fireplace. The kitchen. She saw dark glistening wood and more counter space than she could have ever imagined topped with brown-and-buff-swirled marble. The hardwood floors gleamed while the copper canopy over the huge stove gave a rustic feel and brought out the veins of dark gold in the countertops. A pan holder above the long work space in the center of the room was filled with copper pots. The designers had utilized brick in the spaces between the cabinets, all blending perfectly and framing the glass-enclosed eating nook that offered the same view of the rolling hills outside. Which went on as far as the eye could see. And it all belonged to the Masters family. It was mind-blowing. And it drove home the enormous difference between the Masterses and everyone else.

As odd as it seemed, she'd never consciously made that realization before. As a child, things had just been the way they were. She had never placed any significance on anyone's wealth or standing within the community. People were people and you either liked them or you didn't. Against the majestic background of the ranch and this great house on the hill, suddenly her small home and equally small clinic that she had worked hard to attain became as insignificant as one blade of grass on the ninety-two-thousand-acre ranch.

She heard footsteps coming down the stairs. Chance walked into the kitchen wearing only jeans, his broad shoulders and sculptured chest and abs standing out in stark relief. "Are you thirsty?" He didn't stop until he stood in front of the fridge. "Want a beer? Coke? Lemonade?"

"Lemonade sounds great. Thanks."

Chance popped the tab and handed her the ice-cold can, then grabbed a beer for himself.

"Let's sit." He nodded toward the round oak and black wrought iron table in the breakfast area.

Holly selected a chair and settled Emma on her lap. Chance pulled out a chair, scooting it some distance from where they sat before sitting down.

"You looked good on your gelding." He took a sip of his beer. "How did you ever get started on the dressage thing?"

"I've always been curious about it. Last year I went with Amanda and one of her friends to a competition in Dallas. I was fascinated. Then I met Mark's wife when she brought their dogs into the clinic and we talked. Found out he has been a major contender for years. He helped me get Sinbad."

"And when you're in that English saddle, you control all that power." A sparkle of humor danced in Chance's eyes. "And I would imagine taking him over the jumps flings you up then slams you down when he lands."

"How did you ever know?" Obviously Chance had figured out what she was speaking of that night in the barn.

"And now you throw sin into the mix. A guy had better watch out for you."

"You'll never see me coming."

Chance barked out a laugh and shook his head.

Emma began to whimper, wanting to get down. Holly placed her on the Spanish-tiled floor and away she went—directly to Chance.

"So what's up?"

Chance's eyes were glued to the baby, who held on to a fold in his jeans with one hand and patted his knee with the other. She was doing a little hop dance, wanting to be picked up. Either Chance didn't understand or he was ignoring her. Emma was grinning, those two bottom teeth clearly in sight, so she wasn't distressed either way.

"Cole and Wade are throwing some kind of party in Dallas. Saturday night. I can't get out of it." He looked from the baby to Holly. "I need a date. Would you consider?"

Chance was asking her on a date? She didn't know whether to be elated or frightened. It was something, as a child, she'd thought about. But in a few weeks he would be gone. He was a soldier. His SEAL team was his family. And this was, after all, just one date.

This party would, presumably, have a lot of at-tendees. They would want to talk to Chance and find out what he could tell them of his success on the battlefield. Or if most were friends and asso-ciates of Wade and Cole, the talk would eventu-ally turn to business. Either way, she would be a shadow in a corner somewhere, there only if Chance needed her.

But it was one date. One evening. She could do it. She would do it. How could she not?

"Sure. I would love to. How dressy will it be?"

"Haven't a clue. And I don't much care. We will probably stay overnight, so bring a change of clothes. Any way you want to dress will be fine."

"Will I get a hot dog grilled by your chef?"

The light danced in his eyes. "I never figured that one out, either. But if that's what you want, consider it done."

By the end of the week, Holly was a nervous wreck. She'd be lying if she tried to convince herself otherwise. Amanda had joyfully agreed to keep Emma, saying she was proud of Holly for finally agreeing to go out on a date, comparing it in importance to buying a new house. Granted, she hadn't accepted many invitations, because she hadn't wanted to leave Emma. Not that she felt she'd given up all that much when she'd politely refused other offers. This time was different. This time it was Chance.

"Okay, have you got everything?" Amanda stood in the hall just outside Holly's bedroom door.

"There really isn't that much to take." Shrugging her shoulders, she once again looked at her reflection in the mirror. The strapless black dress clung to every curve of her body, from her breasts to her hips. Just past her waist, varying tones of gray were layered to midthigh. Black heels capped it off.

"You look hot." Amanda grinned. "A bit different from your customary jeans and boots. Chance's eyes are probably going to bug out of his head when he sees you."

"Yeah, right." She swung Emma up in her

arms and walked to the living room. "I appreciate the loan of the dress and the shoes, Mandy."

"Not a problem. Has Chance ever seen you in a dress?"

Holly took a second to think about the question. "No. I don't think he ever has."

She put Emma in the playpen, making sure she had plenty of toys and her juice.

Amanda hurried over to her purse and withdrew a small bottle of perfume. "We almost forgot this." Before Holly could say no, the fragrance floated in the air around her.

"I don't wear perfume."

"Tonight you do." Amanda smiled in smug triumph.

There was a knock on the back door. Chance was here to pick her up. Grabbing the black clutch and a small overnight bag, she walked to the door.

"Hi." She welcomed him in.

"Wow." His eyes traveled over her from her head to her feet. "Actually, I'm here to pick up Holly… Is she here?"

"Very funny."

He took her bag. "You look amazing. Thanks for doing this."

"My pleasure. And you look amazing yourself." He was wearing his full dress whites, with a number of medals pinned on his chest. Not surprising.

"Since this debacle is the work of my brothers, primarily Wade, in an attempt to lure future business associates into his web, he wants to trot out a SEAL. So I'll give him the whole show. But this is it. Never again."

Holly had anticipated that a drive into Dallas would take a couple of hours. When Chance turned left toward the barn, in the opposite direction from the main road, she sat up and took notice. Where was he going? Over one hill and up another and they were parking in front of the hangar at the ranch airport. Chance was out of the car in a heartbeat and had her door opened, offering his hand before she could come to grips with what this meant. They most likely were not driving to Dallas. The thought of flying there had never crossed her mind.

He held her hand as they crossed to the other

side of the asphalt runway where two white-and-blue helicopters sat on their round concrete helipad.

"Are you kidding me?"

"Nope."

She stopped but he didn't let go of her hand. "I'm not getting into that."

Chance tilted his head and pursed his lips. "Why not?"

"I'm not a bird. Do I look like I have feathers? If I die, I don't want to be twenty thousand feet above the ground when it happens."

"You won't be that high, but if you're dead, what difference will it make?"

Holly glared at him. "You know what I mean."

"Come on. It'll be all right." She still wasn't moving. He looked down into her eyes, then brought his hands to cup her face. Before she could grasp his intentions, his lips briefly touched hers. "I would never put you in a dangerous situation. Do you believe that?"

"Yes. I guess I do." She looked up at him, frowning. "Although you are the one who said it would be safe to cross that new bull's pasture to get to the river quicker. That sucker almost ate our lunch."

Chance pulled a hand down over his mouth. She knew she had him there.

"But no one was hurt."

"Only because old man Reichter saw what was happening and released those two heifers into the pasture to distract him."

"Come on. This is not a bull."

"And you've driven one of these before?"

He nodded, taking her hand. "A couple of times. Yeah. What *is* that perfume?" he asked as he settled her into her seat. "It's amazing."

"I don't know. Amanda just grabbed the bottle and dabbed—"

"Find out the name." His eyes sparkled dangerously. "It makes me hungry. Come on. You can do this."

Chance made sure she was buckled in. Once inside, he handed her a headset with a mic before putting on his own.

"Ready?"

"No."

He grinned. That charming, seductive, devil-may-care, bad-boy smile complete with dimples made it no contest. He would win this battle. The engine began turning the rotor blades, faster and faster until she felt the helicopter lift and move forward.

"Wait! Stop!"

Chance looked at her and lowered the chopper back onto the ground. "What's the matter?"

"I wasn't ready. You didn't say we would take off so soon."

He spared her a look clearly saying, *Are you kidding me?* "Holly, get ready. We are going to the moon. Is there anything else?"

"Where are the parachutes?"

"There are no parachutes."

Her eyes got big. "Then, what do we use if we crash?"

"Ah… That would be the ground. Hold on."

With a shake of his head, they were off yet again. The chopper climbed high as Chance circled the ranch then headed south.

"Holly, loosen up. You have a death grip on the seat."

"I think I'm going to be sick."

"No, you aren't. Relax and enjoy the flight."

She nodded, scooted as far away from the outside door as her seat would allow, and in a show of bravery, managed to pry her fingers off the leather seat. Her hands found each other in her lap and she held on tight. The warmth of Chance's hand covered hers, and only then did she begin to relax.

She had to admit, it was an amazing sight. The closer they got to Dallas, the more roads there were and the busier it was. It was twilight, so the sun had set, but darkness hadn't fully taken over. The lights of the city began to come on and it was amazing.

She glanced at Chance. He was so capable, so incredible. He caught her look and winked. "We're ahead of schedule. Do you want to circle Dallas?"

Holly knew this was the chance of a lifetime. When would she ever again be in a helicopter? *Put your fear in your back pocket and trust Chance.* She looked at him and nodded. "I would love it."

He grinned. "That's my girl."

It was just a turn of phrase, but his words hit her hard just the same. Was she his girl? Would she ever be?

The giant skyscrapers of Dallas unfolded below them. As they circled, Holly spotted Pegasus, the flying red horse. Formerly a symbol of Mobil Oil, it now served as both a symbol of Dallas and a representation of its history.

After circling the downtown area, they headed northeast. The city gave way to beautiful estates. They finally touched down at a small suburban airport.

"We're here."

Chance killed the motor and helped her from the chopper, grabbing her overnight bag and handing her the small purse. Just ahead was a stretch limo, the driver patiently waiting next to the car. Placing his hand on the back of her waist, Chance guided her to the vehicle.

This was a day of firsts. While she'd seen limos in and around the big house at the ranch most of her life, she'd never been close to one let alone *in* one. Even when Jason died, a military-issue sedan had picked her up at the airport and taken her to Arlington Cemetery, where her brother had been buried with full honors.

"Since this is our first official date…" Chance said, looking straight ahead as the chauffeur started the limo and drove out onto the highway. Then he turned toward her. "I would like to kiss you."

"I would like that very much."

Chance leaned toward her, put his arm around her shoulders and lowered his head. She felt his hand press against her face, turning her to him. Then his mouth covered hers, his tongue seeking permission to enter, which she happily gave. Typical of Chance, his kiss, like the rest of him, was strong and decisive. He tasted of brandy, a hint of peppermint and his own unique masculine flavor. She again felt the heat in her lower regions. A single thought crossed her mind that if they didn't stop, they were definitely going to be late for his party.

Chance raised his head, separating their lips, but seemed to hesitate as though he'd been forced to stop. His thumb lightly moved over her bottom lip, swollen and moist from his kiss.

"We're here," he said, his voice coarse and deep.

"Oh."

The limo turned into a driveway, coming to a stop in front of tall black wrought iron gates. They opened immediately, and the limo proceeded up the hill and to the right, where a circle drive dipped under a high portico. It was the largest house she'd ever seen. She was certain of that. A mansion complete with turrets made of stone and brick with blooming vines clinging to the mortar, which made it appear more castle than house.

"Is this where Wade lives?" The sheer colossal size of it required confirmation.

Chance nodded as the driver opened his door. "And Cole also stays here when he is in town."

She leaned toward the window and glanced up at the top of the turreted roof then back to Chance. "Promise me the dragons are securely locked in the basement."

He looked at her with surprise. One eyebrow lifted higher than the other, then he pursed his lips as he fought not to laugh. "You know, I'm not entirely sure anyone remembered to do that. We might have a problem."

She drew back and saw the teasing glitter in his steel-blue eyes. She also saw the need.

"Damn, Holly." And his mouth returned to hers, hard, almost frantic as if he wanted to taste all he could before circumstances forced them apart. He was so masculine. He reeked of sex appeal. His lips were unexpectedly tender yet firm. His mouth widened over hers as his tongue deepened its penetration. She felt the sizzle of heat shoot down her spine, pooling in her belly as she melted into him.

A light tap on the glass brought reality creeping back. When Chance hesitantly pulled away, Holly saw Wade standing outside the car window, his brown eyes glittering in amusement. Apparently deciding now was appropriate, he opened the door, bent down and looked past Holly at his brother. "We have rooms upstairs. Shall I tell the guests you'll be a little late?"

"No," Holly answered before Chance. She could feel the deep blush cover her face and neck.

Then Chance's lips were near her ear, his hot

breath causing shivers over her already heated skin. "He's messing with you. But if you change your mind, there are, in fact, rooms available."

"Stop. Both of you!" She laughed. Grabbing Wade's offered hand, she stepped out of the car.

"Wow." Wade held her hands and stepped back for a better overall look. "Holly, you are stunning."

"Thank you. I just hope I don't fall flat on my face in these crazy shoes."

Wade's deep laughter followed her and Chance into the entrance hall.

Holly looked back at him and mouthed the word *What?* which only served to renew his laughter.

The only words to describe the inside of the home were *palatial elegance.* This place made even the big house at the ranch small in comparison. Three-story ceilings, crystal chandeliers, glass walls, steps leading to still more luxury. A huge indoor terrarium dominated one vast corner. Holly had never seen anything like it. They continued through the marble-and-glass foyer and into a huge living room to the right and a dining room that could easily seat forty people on her left. A man in a white jacket offered to take her overnight bag. Chance whispered something in his ear, received an "Of course, sir," and the man hurried away with her bag.

By now some of the guests had begun to notice their arrival. At least they'd realized Chance was there. In his full navy dress whites that served as a backdrop for the medals that almost covered the left side of his broad chest, he was the target of every wannabe macho male and lusty female in the entire house. The music from discreetly hidden speakers blended with the sounds of laughter and excited voices.

"Let's get this over with," Chance whispered to Wade, who stood next to them.

"Ladies and gentlemen." Wade's baritone voice carried through the den of people. Everyone turned and a hush fell over the crowd. The eyes quickly deflected from Holly to Chance. The smiles grew bigger, the eyes brighter, and it seemed as though everyone in the room advanced toward them at the same time. Toward Chance, more specifically.

"Thank you all for coming. I'm delighted to introduce my brother, Lieutenant Commander Chance Masters, US Navy, Special Forces Division, and his close friend Dr. Holly Anderson. Please join me in making them welcome."

There was united applause. Holly knew it was for Chance. She took a few steps back and brought her hands together for Chance. A receiving line formed, everyone anxious to meet Chance and thank him for his service. She felt out of place big-time. This was his night to shine. And he deserved all the accolades these people were willing to bestow.

A waiter in a white coat walked through the crowd carrying a tray filled with champagne flutes. Holly grabbed two and handed one to Chance. There were several hundred people clustered around him. He hadn't mentioned there would be this many people. Maybe he hadn't known. The music filtered into the room, mixing with excited banter. Twice Holly tried to make her escape but found her arm seized and held securely in Chance's hand before she could take one step. *Did the man have eyes in the back of his head?* Eventually most of the people had come forward and introduced themselves, all adding questions about the SEALs, Iraq, BUDS training or the Masters Corporation. Chance said a lot of words that told them nothing. She was amazed at how he could do that.

"I'm starved," he said after the last group had finally dissipated. Taking her hand in his, Chance led her toward the buffet. While he filled his plate with various meat and cheese selections, Holly went for the fruit: bite-size slices of melons, strawberries, cherries and grapes. Then it was finding a place to sit down and eat. With well over three hundred people in attendance, no chairs were available in the living or dining areas.

"We can just stand up," Holly offered.

"I have an idea. Follow me."

Back out in the great hall, Chance walked toward the back of the house. Before they got to the kitchen, he turned into a small alcove on their left. Probably intended as a smaller, more intimate dining room, there was no table or chairs, just one lone sofa and a small flat-screen TV on the opposite wall. The far end of the room was glass panels, giving a view of a large fountain in a garden outside.

Holly walked to the couch and was unable to hold back a sigh of relief when she sank down into the plush leather. By the time Chance joined her, she'd already kicked off the four-inch heels. They ate in unison, enjoying the quiet.

"So do you know all those people?"

"Nope."

"Who was that brunette who was so determined to get close to you? She actually tried to step on my foot in an attempt to make me back away."

"You're kidding." Chance looked from his plate to Holly. There was a frown of concern on his handsome face.

"No. Not kidding." She took a bite of a strawberry. "But no worries. Every time she tried it, I just poked her in the ribs. Oh, these strawberries are so good."

Chance laughed out loud. "You're priceless."

"I'm ornery."

"That, too."

She adjusted her body into a more comfortable position. Doing so caused her plate to tilt. Before she could catch it, a cherry slid off, rolled over Chance's leg and onto the leather of the couch, stopping at his crotch. She looked at him with dismay. He bit down hard, his eyes dancing. Which told her he was going to have fun with this one.

"You uh…lost your cherry, Ms. Anderson," he said, trying to keep a straight face.

"So it would seem," she replied, stiffening her spine, unable to keep from staring at the small red piece of fruit. "Would you be a gentleman and hand it to me?"

"Nope. You'll have to get it yourself."

Holly looked around, making sure no one else was within hearing distance. "Chance Masters," she said through gritted teeth. "Do not do this. This isn't the place or the time. Give me my cherry."

"You want the cherry? Reach down and get it."

The bad-boy light was dancing in his eyes. He was enjoying this way too much.

"Fine. I'll just leave it there and you'll have a stain on your pants."

"Dry cleaners can get it out," he said, sounding totally unconcerned.

Chance reached out to her plate and picked up one of the two remaining pieces of fruit. With his fingers he removed the stem and brought a green grape to her mouth. She opened to accept it, biting down, enjoying the sweet, juicy flavor. He watched as she chewed. Then he scooped up the last piece of fruit, a small strawberry. This time, he put it to his mouth, his teeth holding it in place.

His eyes glittered in challenge. He wanted her to take it. From his mouth. She could do it. Leaning toward him, Holly touched her lips to his as she bit down on the fruit. She felt his hand come around to the back of her head, holding her to him. With his tongue he made sure the fruit was well into her mouth. It turned into a deep, smoldering kiss until she neither knew nor cared where the strawberry went. Against her lips, Chance murmured, "Get the cherry, Holly. Do it. Do it now."

Eight

"Just remember, Commander. Paybacks are hell," she said against his mouth and felt him smile. As she reached out to retrieve the crimson fruit at his crotch, his lips again found hers. He pressed her hand against his swollen erection. The fruit was forgotten. His hard body pushed up against her hand, his own hand pressing hers down on his thickness.

Someone cleared their throat. It wasn't her. It wasn't Chance. All movement came to a screeching halt. Reality flooded into the little room. Chance drew back and she looked up to find Wade standing in the opening next to a chef, who for all intents and purposes appeared as though he wished he was anywhere else. So did Holly. The heat of a deep red blush crept up her face.

"We couldn't find you two." Wade was trying so hard not to grin it would, without doubt, do damage to his facial muscles. "Chef Andre has something for you."

Holly looked at the silver tray in the chef's hand. He lowered it and removed the silver dome cover. It held a hot dog in a bun with an assortment of relishes and condiments on the side.

"As requested, madam. Grilled over an open fire. For you."

He held the tray toward them. Thankfully Chance reached out and took it. Her hands were shaking so badly she would have probably dumped the whole plate in his lap. A new rush of heat ran up her neck and face as an image flashed in her mind of how Chance would ask her to clean that up. This had to stop.

"Thank you."

"You are quite welcome. I hope you enjoy," Chef said before turning away.

"Something is begging me to ask what you

both were up to when I walked in here," Wade said. "But, nah. I don't think I really need to ask, do I? And if I did, you probably wouldn't tell me, would you?"

"Honestly, Wade. It's all just a big misunderstanding." Holly would not leave him thinking she'd come to his elaborate party just to make out with his brother. Even though she had been doing just that. There was a distinct difference between making out and *making out*. "What you saw was not really representative of what we were doing."

Chance snorted and she sent a glare in his direction.

"Oh?" Wade's dark eyes glimmered with barely contained amusement.

She shook her head. "I was simply helping Chance find my cherry."

No one moved.

It took about five seconds to realize what she'd said.

Her admission didn't faze Chance as he dangled the small red fruit from its stem.

"And I got it," he said, before popping it in his mouth, grinning like the Cheshire cat.

The hot dog was delicious, and in spite of having already eaten all that fruit, she downed every bite. Chance disappeared for a couple of minutes and was soon back with a lemonade and a cold beer.

"Wade is offering his guests beer? That seems a little odd."

"He keeps them in the fridge. I never really formed a liking for champagne."

Holly took a sip of her lemonade. Neither had she, but probably not for the same reasons. People on her side of the road generally didn't attune their taste buds to the full-flavored bouquet of the world's finest champagne.

"What now?" she asked, setting her empty plate aside.

"Put your shoes on and I'll show you."

Stifling a groan, she stood up and slipped her feet into the shoes. Chance took her hand and led her to a large room adjacent to the atrium. Above them there was a dome ceiling decorated with twinkle lights. At the back of the room a six-piece orchestra was tuning up. As the music filled the space, Chance took Holly into his arms.

"This is so nice," she said, smiling up at him. "I didn't know you danced."

"You're about to find out I don't. Watch your toes."

He danced beautifully. It felt so good to be held in his strong arms, pulled tight against his powerful body as they swayed to the strings of the slow, soul-touching melody.

As they danced it felt as though the temperature in the room got warmer. The songs being played now were slower, the melodies strumming the strings of her heart. Holly felt as though she'd stepped up to an entirely new level, feeling a closeness to Chance she'd never felt before. There were plenty of women at the edge of the dance floor who were ready to pounce and take her place at the first opportunity, but selfishly she held on tight. And it seemed Chance was equally unwilling to release Holly.

"When you're ready to call it a night and head upstairs, just let me know. We've been here over four hours. I'm more than ready to get the hell out of here."

Holly stepped back. "Let's go."

He took her hand and led her through the throngs of people still making the most of the party. Just outside the double doors that opened into the great hall, they found Cole.

Chance leaned forward and quietly spoke a few words to his brother, who nodded and gave Chance a couple of pats on the back. Cole looked at Holly and winked.

Then Chance guided her farther down the hall to a small elevator. A couple of seconds later they stepped out onto a higher floor. It was peacefully quiet and every bit as elegant as the first floor had been. These people knew how to live. Antique mirrors randomly adorned the walls along the hallway. In between were very old, beautifully framed pictures, presumably of Chance's ancestors. Men standing with a crowd of smiling people in front of the entrance to a mine, next to an oil rig or next to a gorgeous thoroughbred held by a groomsman with a jockey on its back and a blanket of roses over its neck.

"That's my uncle on the day he won the Triple Crown."

"He's magnificent."

"I assume you mean the horse?"

"There's a horse?"

Chance laughed and it was a nice sound to hear.

"I think you'll be comfortable in here." He pushed open the door to an amazing bedroom suite. It was decorated in varying shades of blue in a French motif with a fireplace on one wall. A large canopy bed dominated the room. "I'll be just next door."

"Okay. I'll see you in the morning."

"I'm an early riser."

"So am I."

Chance leaned down, his face close to hers. The dim lighting in the hall shadowed just enough of his features to make him devilishly handsome.

"I had a good time," she whispered.

"I can almost say the same. You made it bearable. Thank you, Holly."

Then his lips, gentle, sweeping, were joining

hers. He ventured inside just enough to taste and let her do the same. Then he was pulling back.

"Good night."

"So did you have fun?" Amanda asked the next day as Holly sat holding Emma, bouncing her on her lap. She couldn't kiss the baby enough, hold her tight enough. The fragrance of baby powder, shampoo and Emma was a much-needed relaxant after her overnight stay in Dallas. She now knew how Cinderella had felt going to the ball. Thankfully Holly had returned home intact— with both shoes. And the great blue-and-white flying coach had made a perfect landing with the prince behind the controls.

"Holly?"

"Oh. Yes!" Holly came back to reality. "Sorry. Just a bit jet-lagged."

"Jet-lagged? You only went to Dallas. This just keeps getting better. I'm going to want to hear all about it. Every delicious savory detail. Promise me."

"Sure." *Not.*

"Okay, then. I've gotta head out. I'll talk with you soon."

"Thanks so much, Amanda." Holly stood and hugged her friend's neck. "Really. You are so great to keep the baby for me."

"Anytime." Amanda touched the tip of Emma's nose. "See ya, kiddo."

"Keyo."

Holly saw Amanda to the door, then called Kevin. She and Emma checked the clinic and made sure all was in order for tomorrow. Monday. Always a busy day.

Something woke Holly out of a sound sleep. The dogs in the kennel were barking in that way dogs do when there is someone or something in their immediate vicinity. Two shepherds, a terrier and a mixed breed named Henry were definitely acknowledging something.

She slipped out of bed, tiptoed across the hall and into Emma's room. The baby was sleeping peacefully. About the time she returned to the hallway, the sound of breaking glass reached her ears and the dogs were now going crazy. It sounded as though it was coming from the clinic.

Pulling on a pair of jeans, she slipped into her shoes and stepped out into the cool night air. She hadn't gone but a few steps when the back door to the building swung open. The security lights, one on each end of the clinic, had been turned off. From the small amount of moonlight, she saw the darkly clad figure throwing something out. It crashed when it hit the ground. Her computer?

Holly turned and ran back inside the house, making sure the door was locked behind her. She didn't want to turn on any light to draw attention. Grabbing the cell phone from the kitchen counter where it was charging, she quickly called 911. The dispatcher answered immediately. Holly quickly gave her name, address and the reason for her call and was assured the police would be sent right away.

Ending the call, she slipped her cell into the pocket of her jeans and hurried to Emma's room. More sounds of glass shattering and continued barking tore open the night. It was over fifteen miles to town. Chance was across the road. Without giving it a second thought, Holly dialed his cell. He picked up on the second ring.

"Holly?" His voice sounded amazingly awake for two o'clock in the morning.

"Chance, I think someone is in the clinic. I've called the police but Emma and I are here alone and—"

The connection went dead.

Returning to the front room, Holly peeked through the blinds behind the sofa. From here she could see the back of the clinic. Suddenly light from a vehicle flashed across the window. She heard a door slam, and seconds later the driver ran in front of the lights toward the clinic's front door. It must have been Chance.

Immediately she regretted calling him. If someone was in there, the person might have a gun. She couldn't bear to think she might be the cause of Chance getting seriously injured. She couldn't leave Emma alone so all she could do was watch and wait. Someone in dark clothing ran out the side door they used for deliveries but it was too dark to make out more than a shadow.

Seconds later the back door to the clinic opened and Chance lumbered out through it, making a straight line for her house. Holly quickly ran to her back door and opened it.

"Are you okay?"

"Yes. Was someone in there?"

"Definitely. But they got out before I could get in there. My truck lights probably warned them I was coming."

"Them?"

"Them. Him. I don't know, but there is a lot of damage for just one person to do."

"Damage?" Holly reached for the door. "How much damage?"

"No, Holly." Chance kept her from going outside. "We don't know how many there were. We don't know why. And we don't know if it's safe. I cleared all the rooms but whoever did this might be lurking in the wooded area between the clinic and your house."

"The dogs. I've got to at least make sure the dogs are okay."

"How many?"

"Four."

"I saw them and they all appeared okay. I'll go back and check them again when the police get here."

Before she could voice an objection she heard the sound of a siren. Officers from the Calico County sheriff's office were on the way. Once they arrived and checked inside and out, Holly was allowed to go into the clinic. It looked as if somebody had set out to destroy everything possible. Expensive microscopes had been thrown through walls. X-ray screens were on the floor in pieces. There was no sign of her computer, which probably meant she was correct to think it was lying in pieces outside.

It definitely wasn't someone trying to steal and resell. It was vandalism with a vengeance. She hurried down the hall to the kennel, switching on the lights. One by one she checked the animals for any cuts or indications they were hurt. They were all fine. Still excited, but fine.

"Holly." John Green, a deputy for the county, called her back to the main part of the clinic, where Chance stood. "Do you have any idea who might have done this?"

Holly shook her head. "No. Not at all. Most of our patients are healthy and happy. I've only lost two. A seventeen-year-old beagle belonging to J.D. Cordiff. But Mr. Cordiff is in his eighties. He understood his dog had health issues no vet could cure. And Sammy Bartlett lost his Bubbles to cancer a week ago. Sammy is seven. I know his parents. No way they would ever do anything like this. I can't think of anyone who would have done this or why. Excuse me, I've got to go and check on Emma."

As Holly hurried back to the house, she couldn't stop the tears from welling in her eyes. Who would do such a thing? And why? Thankfully insurance would cover most of the loss, but even then it would take weeks to get back up and running. She needed to call Kevin.

Emma was still sleeping soundly in her bed, snuggling her stuffed goat. Holly took the cell from her pocket and speed-dialed Kevin's number. She probably should wait until the morning, but this was serious. It would impact his family's earnings. After three rings, she heard Kevin's sleepy voice on the other end of the line.

After explaining what had happened and hanging up, Holly ventured back outside. She wasn't sure what to think or where to begin. Walking back to the clinic, she began picking up pieces of her equipment. Broken monitor frames, a smashed keyboard, the frame of a very expensive microscope Wade had given as a grand opening gift.

"Holly." Chance reached out to her, taking the shattered pieces of various instruments from her hand, tossing it all to the ground then drawing her into his arms. "Leave it until the morning. You don't need to be out here trying to clean up in the dark. The sheriff is going to keep one unit out here overnight. I've already called and arranged for a couple of ranch hands to keep them company just in case."

She nodded. "I called Kevin. He's going to contact the insurance company. Maybe they will send someone out fairly quickly. Oh, Chance, I have patients who need medical attention. How am I ever…"

"Shh." Chance's hand gently pressed her head against his chest, keeping her close. "We will get through this. One step at a time. I want you to go inside your house and get Emma. Pack a few things for both of you. You're coming to my house until the authorities can get a handle on what's doing."

"No, that isn't necessary. We'll be fine…"

"I intend to make sure. Go. Pack a bag and let's get you out of here."

"But, Chance—"

"Now, Muppet. Stop arguing and go. There is no way you're staying in that isolated house tonight." He stepped back and with his finger, raised her face to his. "You can save that stubborn set of the jaw and battle stance for when they catch the perp. This is one argument you will not win."

She turned and walked toward her house. Chance wouldn't leave her out here in a wooded area with no alarm system and no way to defend herself. Even though a couple of sheriff's deputies and a few of the cowboys were stationed in the area, he would not let her stay here tonight. She supposed there was some logic to it. She had to think of Emma. But what she really wanted to do was hide somewhere and wait for the vandal or vandals to come back. Her shock was rapidly changing into anger.

"Pick any bedroom you want. Wade and Cole are in Dallas so it's just us." He stepped over to the outside wall and flipped open a small, discreetly hidden panel. Punching a few numbers, he then shut the lid. "Security. Tonight I don't trust anything. Come on, you're exhausted. Lets get you and the baby upstairs."

"I'm not exhausted," Holly retorted. "I'm mad as hell."

To that, Chance could only smile. When Holly had initially called, it had frightened him. Something that didn't happen very often. He had heard the fear mixed with fury in her tone. He had a feeling were it not for the baby, Holly would have jumped right in the middle of the situation, confronting whoever it was destroying her clinic, and God only knew what would have happened then. She'd never been afraid of very much of anything; whether that was an admirable trait or a fool's mission he wouldn't say. But before

tonight, he'd respected it. Now he was just glad
the baby had instilled a degree of protective cau-
tion in her.

He followed Holly up the stairs. She stopped at
the top as though lost and unsure of what to do
next. Chance stepped forward and opened a door
to one of the bedrooms next to his. She walked
past him, still holding the baby, checking it out.
During the day, the view from here framed the
barn and various outbuildings. Step out on the
balcony and it had a good view of the courtyard
below and the pool with the waterfall.

Seeing Holly inside this house affected him
in ways he didn't want to think about. In all the
years they'd known each other, she'd never ventured farther into the home than the kitchen and
den downstairs. Now, seeing her in a bedroom,
a king-size bed three feet away from where she
stood, did something to his equilibrium. For just
an instant he let himself envision Holly lying in
the center of that bed wrapped in his arms, the
sheets tangled around their legs while he took
her again and again.

Chance was doing it again. He was envisioning

something that could never happen. He needed to stop.

"I asked a couple of men to bring the baby's bed over." He was prepared for her objections and raised his hands, palms out. "It's just for a couple of nights. I thought you both might sleep better. You won't have to spend the night worrying that she might fall off the bed, and I think she'll be more at ease in her own bed, with her toys. It might help to comfort her." Holly was not going back to her little house until a good security system had been installed. But he didn't want to add that argument to the problems she already faced. At least not tonight. If there was luck to be had, it would be a done deal before she knew anything about it.

By now Emma was awake, her eyes as big as saucers as she took in her new surroundings, her first finger getting quite a chewing. Holly let her down to wander around and she made a beeline for Chance. She was so tiny. So innocent. He was afraid to pick her up for fear he would hurt her, but apparently the child had different ideas. She looked up into his face, her blue eyes asking a silent question while she gripped the pant leg of his jeans in her tiny hand.

"Up," she said with absolute clarity.

Chance glanced at Holly. She just smiled. If he didn't know better he would swear she had set him up. Feeling uneasy, Chance reached down and picked up the baby. She immediately laid her head against his shoulder, her hand gripping his shirt, settling in as though she had always slept there. He gently patted her back with his free hand. He couldn't believe how right she felt in his arms. He wouldn't admit, even to himself, how much he liked holding her.

"I imagine the sheriff will try to lift some fingerprints from your clinic tomorrow. I know over half the town has been inside the building, but maybe he'll get lucky in the lab area. I assume not everyone goes back there."

"No, they don't." She shrugged.

A rap outside the door drew their attention. "Got the little one's bed, boss. Where you want it?" Two of the ranch hands looked inside the bedroom, finally turning to Chance for directions.

"Just put it… You know, I guess you'd better put it close to the bed so if she wakes up she can see her mother."

The two stout cowboys soon had the bed sitting next to the large bed where Holly would sleep. With a tip of their hat, they said good-night and left the room.

"You really didn't have to do this. It's a lot of trouble for one night."

"No big deal." Chance walked to the baby's bed and deposited Emma in it. She immediately sat up and looked around, her pointer finger securely in her mouth. "See you tomorrow."

"Thank you." Holly sat on the edge of her bed and stared at the baby. If he had a guess, he'd bet she wouldn't sleep tonight.

Chance nodded, closed the bedroom door behind him and headed for the stairs. He wanted to take another look at the clinic and see if he could pick up on anything he may have overlooked the first time when he was hurrying to try to catch the perp. The clinic might be a target for whatever drugs she kept on hand, but the damage done was far and above just someone looking for drugs. Somebody wanted to do damage. A lot of damage.

Nodding to the deputy standing guard at the front entrance of the clinic, Chance again looked at the damage covering the counters and floor.

"Have you checked the fridge?" he asked the deputy. "I was thinking this might be about narcotics."

"Yes, sir," the officer respectfully replied. "We haven't checked each item off a list but it appears that area of the lab was about the only part untouched. I had the same thought that it was somebody looking for drugs, but apparently not. This whole thing is really strange." He looked at Chance. "I've known Kevin most of my life. Both he and Holly were very organized. In the drawer containing sedatives and pain relievers not one vial was out of place, no bottles turned over. So more than likely this wasn't about pharmaceuticals or theft. That narrows the suspects considerably."

Yes, Chance thought as he bid the officer goodnight. It certainly did.

When he returned to the ranch house, he reset

the alarm and went upstairs to check on Holly. When a knock on the bedroom door didn't get an answer, he opened it. The room was dark. The ambient light let him see that the baby was again sound asleep. Holly had removed her jeans and boots, but she still sat on the side of the bed, clad in a T-shirt, her hands folded in her lap. He couldn't see her face, but he would bet she was crying. For someone who had worked so long and hard to accomplish her dream, to find it trashed must have been devastating.

"Holly?" He walked toward the bed.

"Who would do that, Chance?" Her voice was so soft he had to strain to hear. "They weren't hurting me. They were taking away medical care for dozens of innocent animals. Who would do that?"

"I don't know, but eventually the sheriff will figure it out."

She couldn't sit like this all night. She'd had a shock and needed to get some sleep. He walked to the far side of the bed and pulled down the covers.

"Come on. Climb in and try to go to sleep."

As though hypnotized, she stood and walked around to that side of the bed. He covered her with the comforter and turned to leave.

"Will you stay?"

Chance hesitated. "I'm not sure that would be a good idea."

Holly nodded and looked down at her hands. Shit. Under the circumstances, how could he say no?

"Scoot over next to Emma's bed."

When she complied, he removed his boots and lay down on top of the bedding. He understood her need for his presence. The break-in made her feel as though she herself had been attacked. She felt unsafe and vulnerable.

For maybe the first time in his adult life, he stretched out on a bed next to a beautiful woman and sex never entered his mind.

Nine

Mondays were always busy. This one was insanity. The pet owners she couldn't reach showed up with their dogs and cats and iguanas and pigs to be told the clinic was closed. The more severe cases were referred to the clinic in the next county.

By nine o'clock the police were doing their follow-up inspection, inside and out. Holly sat outside under a tree answering the phone while Kevin spoke with the officers and tried to wrap his mind around the destruction. Amanda, bless her, was at Chance's house with Emma after Chance assured her there was cable and a couple of flat-screens and she could help herself to anything in the kitchen.

A little after two that afternoon the claims adjuster arrived and began the process of assessing the damage so a dollar figure could be determined.

By the end of the day, Holly was exhausted. But Chance had once again stepped into the role of protector and became her rock, just as he had when she was ten and a bully had tried to take her lunch. She noticed even Kevin asked for his opinion several times.

Dinner that evening was prepared by the Masterses' chef on the outdoor grill. It smelled heavenly, making her realize she hadn't eaten all day. But at least the worst was over. New equipment had been ordered and would start arriving tomorrow, again thanks to Chance. Holly had argued vehemently against taking money from him but finally agreed on behalf of the animals and Kevin, whose family depended on the business's income. She did, too, but she also had a small inheritance from Aunt Ida and only Emma to care for, versus three kids and a mortgage. She and Kevin would just sign the insurance check over to Chance when it came. The clinic, while strangely bare, was clean and ready for the new equipment to be installed.

Emma was fretful for the first time Holly could remember.

"What's wrong with her?" Chance asked. "Is she sick?"

"I don't think so," Holly said. "I think it's because she's in strange surroundings. Maybe she's picking up on my emotions."

"You look dead on your feet."

"Yeah. That's pretty close." She tried bouncing Emma on her knees, but to no avail. "I want to thank you for all you've done, Chance. I don't know how any of us would have gotten through it were it not for you." Especially last night, but she wasn't going to bring that up. She wished the circumstances could have been different.

"You would have been fine."

She shook her head but was too tired to argue. "I'm going to take Emma upstairs and see if I can get her to sleep."

"All right. Get some sleep yourself. See you in the morning."

Because of Emma's fussiness, Holly let her play longer than usual in the big bathtub of the en suite where Holly was staying. Story time followed, and finally with a warm bottle of comfort milk, Emma fell asleep.

Holly ditched her dirty clothes and headed back into the bathroom. That jet tub had her name written all over it. Lying back, she let the jets massage away the weariness. An hour later, dressed in clean clothes and feeling a lot better, she jumped in the big bed, hoping tonight she could sleep. But sleep didn't come easy. Chance wasn't here tonight and there was no reason to ask him to be.

Still, the silk sheets felt amazing, especially compared with her sturdy cotton bedding at home. The thick silk comforter made a soft rustling sound when she moved; the fragrance in the room was a beautiful blend of cedar and honeysuckle. All of it served as a heady reminder that she was in the ranch mansion with Chance sleeping steps away.

She must have slept a while but before long, she was again wide-awake. The large house was quiet. Feeling thirsty, Holly slipped out of bed, checked on Emma, who was sleeping peacefully, and headed to the stairs. She should have thought to bring a glass into the bedroom before retiring, but then she rarely became thirsty during the night. It was nerves. Had to be.

The large timber joists crossing the top of the den and on the staircase were amazing from this elevated angle. At the bottom of the stairs she padded into the kitchen, found a glass and filled it with cool tap water.

Sipping the water, she meandered toward the huge den and the French doors that opened out onto the flagstone patio with the giant columns bordering the outside dining area, the lagoon-style pool and the large waterfall in the background. A splash drew her attention. Minutes later Chance's head broke the surface of the water. He began to swim the length of the pool, back and forth, his powerful arms and his muscled legs propelling him at a fast pace. Curiosity got the better of her and she walked up next to the glass panes of the French doors.

He was magnificent, so powerful. Put all the sexier-than-hell ingredients into a bowl and stir. The final product was right in front of her. And his apparent unawareness of how he affected the female species just made it worse. Or better, as it were.

She set her glass on a nearby table, careful to make sure it wouldn't leave a ring. When she looked again, Chance was coming out of the water.

Without one stitch of clothes on that hard, muscular body.

He grabbed a towel and began to dry himself off. Holly realized he was headed for the door, directly in front of where she stood. He was coming inside and she was standing there gawking. He hadn't seen her yet. She turned, intending to make a break for it. But where? She'd waited too late to run up the stairs. There was no place to hide in the kitchen. She spun around and folded herself into the linen draperies framing the French doors.

Holly listened as Chance pulled open the door and closed it behind him. The lights came on in the kitchen. She heard movement. Then the lights went out and all was quiet. Peeking through a slit between two drapery panels, she saw him walking toward the stairs, one thick white towel fisted in his hand. His body was incredible. The muscles in his back moved beneath the tanned skin; his legs were equally well defined.

When he made it three steps up the stairs, he stopped. Holly held her breath. She didn't want to be caught lurking, ogling a naked man, even if it was Chance. Especially if it was Chance. She snapped her head back, closing the tiny gap in the blinds, and made like a statue, barely allowing herself to breathe. After what seemed like hours, she again cautiously moved the panel aside. No sign of him on the stairs. No indication he was in the kitchen. She strained to listen and heard nothing. Feeling assured he must have gone on to another part of the large house, she stepped out from behind the drapery.

"Well, well," he said, standing right next to her, one bulging arm braced on the wall. His gaze held her motionless. His lips pursed as he hid a smile. "It would appear we have a Peeping Tom."

She could feel the deep blush run up her face and back down her neck. "No…no, you don't. Me? You mean *me*? I was just going to the kitchen to get some water." She knew her eyes were as big as saucers. "See?" She pointed to the small occasional table and the glass of water sitting on top.

A few droplets from his hair dripped onto his broad shoulders. She watched them trickle down over his chest.

"The kitchen is over there."

"I know where the kitchen is," she snapped back at him. "You scared me, that's all."

"I scared you? How exactly did I do that?"

"You were in the pool."

"Oh. People swimming frightens you."

"Nobody goes swimming at two o'clock in the morning. Especially without any… Especially outside."

"Especially buck naked?" Yet again, those sexy dimples cracked the surface and that devilish bad-boy look danced in his eyes.

"I didn't say that."

He frowned and sidestepped until he was in front of her, placing his other hand against the wall on the other side of her and leaning in. He tilted his head, as if trying to figure something out. "You're twenty-four. And you're a doctor."

"Almost."

"And you know more about sex than I do. Isn't that what you said? That first night in the barn?"

"I really don't remember."

"Uh-huh. So seeing a naked man cooling off in his own pool is no big deal. Right?"

She shrugged her shoulders, acting nonchalant. "Right." Her chin jutted out as though daring him to contradict it. "So why are you making this such a big deal?"

"Me?" He adjusted his stance. "Sweetheart, I'm not the one hiding in the draperies."

With an unhurried motion, he shook out the towel and draped it around his hips, tucking in the corner. "Better?"

"It doesn't make any difference to me."

"I wouldn't have thought a grown woman—

a *doctor*, no less—would be embarrassed by a little nudity."

"It wasn't a *little* nudity."

He raised his eyebrows and tilted his head once again, suggesting she might want to explain that remark. The devilish light danced in his eyes.

"That's not what I…I mean…" The blush returned, this time twice as strong, covering her face and neck. She even felt her ears burn. "You're twisting what I say."

"How am I doing that?"

Chance ventured closer to her and she couldn't breathe. The awareness overwhelmed her once again, making little prickles dance over her skin, her senses excruciatingly acute.

Placing her hands against his broad chest, she attempted to push him back. Granite boulders the size of her house would be easier to move. His bare skin was cool at first touch but heated to a sweltering glow beneath her hands. "You're in my space," she snapped. "Please move back."

"Why? I like being in your space." A wicked smile turned up the corners of his mouth. "I'll share mine if you'll share yours. Tit for tat. How about that?"

"This is ridiculous. I'm not having this conversation. It's pointless and stupid."

She heard his masculine chuckle as she spun on her toes, ducked under his arm and headed for the stairs.

"Maybe ridiculous is not what you're feeling. Maybe *frustration* is a better description?"

"What's that supposed to mean?" Then she caught herself. She was walking into his web. She raised her hand in a signal of stop. "You know what? I don't want to know. Forget I asked. I'm not having this conversation."

She paused at the bottom of the stairs, feeling a little bit safe now that she was a few feet away from him. "But if it was frustration—and I'm not saying that is true *at all*—you caused it. You probably did it on purpose."

"So hiding in the drapes gawking at a naked man is my fault?" He barked out a laugh.

"You're the SEAL, not me."

Chance frowned and raised his hands to his hips. "You're going to have to explain that one."

"If you weren't a SEAL you would never have known I was in the drapes and none of this would be happening."

With a flip of her hair she again turned toward the stairs. She almost made it to the fourth step before she was scooped into his arms. And as soon as he turned around and crossed the threshold of the French doors, she knew where he was going.

"Don't you dare. Don't you dare even think about it."

He stopped at the edge of the pool. It appeared he was still struggling to contain a smug grin. "Don't you know a SEAL can't resist a dare?"

His face was so close, his handsome features so charismatic. Chance was the epitome of an adult alpha male in every sense of the phrase, by anyone's definition. To be held in his arms, so close she could smell the essence of his body, was a heady sensation.

"Chance. Put me down," she said, choosing her words carefully. "Please."

"Just put you down? That's all you want?"

"Yes."

The grooves on either side of his mouth deepened and the dimples made another appearance. "Bribe me."

The breath caught in her throat.

"What do you want?" she asked, afraid he would say what she wanted to hear.

"You."

A shiver that felt very much like anticipation crawled over her skin. His voice was deep and coarse, sounding as though he was as affected by their closeness as she was.

Her gaze drifted down to his lips. She couldn't stop it.

"But for now, I'll settle for a kiss. It would be a shame to get you wet before you're ready for bed. But—" he frowned in contemplation "—maybe I could help with that, too."

"Put me down."

"Do it, Holly."

"I've already kissed you."

"No. I've kissed *you*. There's a difference. My arms are getting so tired. Hope my strength doesn't give out."

His strength wouldn't give out if he stood here

like this for a week. But with her arms already around his thick neck, she leaned toward him and pressed her lips to his.

"There. Happy? Now please put me down."

The light in his eyes danced wickedly.

"I've had handshakes that were more enticing than that kiss. That wasn't a kiss. It was… You know, I'm not sure what it was." Then in a softer, absolutely mesmerizing whisper, "Let's try it again."

Holly's lips found his like a magnet pulled to a giant piece of steel. It was a hot, intense sensation and she wanted more, especially when the master took over and provided another lesson on how it was done. A small moan escaped and Chance responded, taking her mouth, taking what he wanted.

She knew an instant of breathless elation before he lifted his mouth.

"I think it needs some work."

She was stupefied. "What do you mean it—"

Before she could finish her sentence, she was flying through the air, her mind trying desperately to catch up before she hit the chilling water with a splash. She went down like a floundering goose with a bowling ball tied to its feet. Kicking off from the bottom, she broke the surface sputtering and spewing, still not able to believe what he'd just done. If looks could kill, he would be a dead man.

A large hand reached down to her. With a glare she brushed it aside.

"I would offer you my towel but…"

"Shut. Up."

"Tomorrow night? About the same time?"

Holly made no further remark. She didn't open her mouth. She marched past him, not stopping until she was up the stairs and headed to her room.

"Do you still want something to drink?" Chance called from below.

She stomped down the hall, slinging water as she went. She slammed the door, belatedly remembering the baby. She hoped it didn't wake Emma.

She could still hear his laughter echoing through the house.

Ornery man.

Ten

Chance threw a saddle on the bay he'd ridden a couple of weeks before. He'd tried to call his CO to see if there had been any news on his pending medical decision. He'd had to leave a message and he didn't like doing that. There was no telling when he would get the call. It could be days. He hated the idea of missing it. But he disliked sitting by a phone and waiting for it to ring even more. *Dammit.* He felt fine. He was ready to get back to the SEALs. He was ready to pick up his AK-47 and complete a mission. He needed the focus. He wanted a way to expel some of this pent-up energy that had him bouncing off the walls. He needed his team. They understood. Hell, they might be the only ones who could.

Wade and Cole were making him absolutely crazy. They wanted him working in the company and, Wade at least, wouldn't drop it. The man had looked him right in the face and declared his intent to sell the ranch, knowing what it meant to Chance. And knowing there was probably little to nothing Chance could do to stop it without returning as a partner in the Masters Corporation.

He would like to get his hands on the books. Every question he'd asked about the ranch met a dead end. Wade talked in circles, something he was very good at doing. Were they hiding something? He was used to getting inside intel immediately, and this cat-and-mouse thing Wade had going was making him nuts. Obviously it was a ploy to try to make Chance conform. *Good luck with that.*

Regardless of how long he'd been away, he wasn't some stranger facing Wade over a bargaining table. This wasn't about a corporate takeover or the buying and selling of stocks or companies. It was about his life. And Wade was in line for an eye-opener if he thought he could coerce Chance into leaving the SEALs.

Securing the cinch, he exchanged the halter for a bridle, led the gelding out of the barn and climbed in the saddle. When Chance was younger, this was the way he'd dealt with all the crap he faced on a daily basis. People had their own idea of what the son of a billionaire should act like, talk like, be like. The toughest lesson had been the realization that because somebody said you were a friend, it didn't necessarily mean shit. People always wanted something. Whether it was a claim of friendship, a favor or money, Chance Masters had quickly become the go-to guy.

Living up to the expectations of others was the worst. No one had been willing to accept him for who he was inside. Over the years it soured him until finally, he'd had enough and began to strike back. He would talk and act exactly as people around him expected. If someone wanted a car, hell, he'd help the person steal it. Who cared if they got caught? Certainly not his old man. If somebody dared him, he'd no longer brushed it off and walked away. Fights? Bring it on. Girls? There were two kinds. He'd learned the difference. The innocents, the girls like Holly's sister, he'd given a wide berth. With the others he'd gained a reputation. Love 'em and leave 'em. He didn't care. They used him, so he'd returned the favor. He'd been on a downhill spiral and only two things had saved his ass. The friendship of Jason Anderson and the lynching committee that had finally approached his father and demanded he do something about his son's illicit behavior. He guessed the good citizens of Calico County had finally determined they cherished something more than money, so his father's little payoffs— some called them bribes—had no longer worked.

Passing through the gate leading into the north range, Chance urged the bay into a slow canter. He knew this ranch like the back of his hand. And he knew how to disappear. Let his CO leave a message. Let his brothers find something better to do.

Holly was the one thing he hadn't envisioned when he'd decided to return to the ranch for his mandatory medical leave. He'd known what his brothers would try to do. He'd come up with a plan of what he'd do if any of the old gang wanted a rematch. But he'd never seen Holly coming.

Keeping his hands to himself was a lesson in futility. No matter what he planned or what safeguards he put in place, when she came near he had to touch her. He had to hold her. He had to kiss her. And he wanted to do a hell of a lot more than that. Knowing she would let him because she thought she was in love with him only made it worse. He would soon be leaving, one way or the other, and had no plans to come back. If the MEB granted him active status, he would be on the first flight back to his team. If they didn't, he had a couple of options, but returning to Texas wasn't one of them. He'd had enough. Wade's intentions to sell the ranch had pretty well, pretty effectively driven the stake into his back. And turned it.

Holly was raising a baby. Jason's baby. That small family had already lost enough. Chance damn sure wouldn't put himself in the situation of being responsible for any tiny life. Babies were too fragile. He'd already proved he could not protect a child. The thought had crossed his mind that maybe he could ask Holly to come with him. In how many languages could he say *stupid idea*? She had Jason's daughter and had achieved a lifelong dream of opening a vet clinic. She was less than one year away from obtaining her doctor of veterinary medicine license. She was safe and happy, and no way would he screw that up.

Reaching the top of a small rise, Chance paused to get his bearings and just appreciate the view. The green of the land against the dark blue sky. How often had he wished he could be exactly here when instead he was stretched out on a roof in Pakistan with his sniper rifle, waiting for someone to come out of a house carrying a bomb? And praying it wouldn't be a child.

Chance encouraged his horse to continue forward. A lone cow bellowed in the distance, somewhere a hawk found its meal and an American bald eagle circled overhead. In spite of the vague rumble of thunder in the distance, it couldn't be a more perfect day.

The sound of rushing water and the smell of the river found his senses. Reining the bay to the right, he followed the riverbank. The one place he hadn't visited in too long was his mom's cottage. Heaven help Wade or Cole if anything had happened to it. It was a small house in the trees, sitting back from the river enough to ensure it never flooded. It was where she'd finally found some peace and maybe a small bit of happiness. It was where, when she'd given up on her husband ever coming home and simply loving her, she had spent the last six or seven years of her life. It was where Chance had found her, her thin body still in the rocking chair, a picture of his father clutched against her breast.

Chance had to wonder if Wade—or Cole—had ever seen their mother break down and openly weep because the man she loved never seemed to have time for her. Never gave her the same consideration he gave to a business associate. Chance damn sure had seen it. He'd sat with her while she'd wiped her tears on more than one occasion. Wade and Cole had been away at school. One time he'd sneaked a phone out of the house and called Wade, telling him their mother was not doing well. He didn't know what else to say. When Wade finally did return home, his mother had hid her grief well and his eldest brother had looked at him as if he was crazy.

Did Wade never wonder why the little house had been built out here? Had he asked their mother why she'd moved out of the mansion to spend her remaining days on the earth in that cabin? A blanket of panic and misery had fallen over Chance when he'd realized his mother had finally given up. She'd given up on their father. She'd given up on life. She'd never confided in him, but he'd known. Somehow, he'd known. He actually couldn't remember if their father had come to her funeral. Surely he had. But Chance didn't recall seeing him there. Or in the house before or after the services. But then, Chance hadn't looked very hard.

Holly sat by the pool, keeping an eye on Emma as she alternately played and begged to get out of her playpen. She wanted to shred the plants and

Holly was having no part of it. She was glad to see Amanda's car come up the long drive.

"Well, don't you two ladies look like the privileged elite," Amanda said as she climbed out of her vehicle. She entered the gate and joined Holly, pulling up a padded lawn chair. "So what happened with the clinic?"

"We don't know anything yet. The replacement equipment has been ordered and should be delivered today or tomorrow. Kevin is overseeing that. I know how to read a slide under a microscope, but how to connect a microscope to the computer is beyond me."

"Well, look at it this way. You weren't going to get any time off for a couple of years. You should make the best of it."

Holly nodded. "You're right."

"And this—" Amanda held out her arms to indicate where they sat "—is not a bad way to start."

Amanda was right. There was only one main ingredient missing.

"Hi, Emma." Amanda stood and walked to the

playpen, picking up the baby when she raised her arms.

"Don't let her near the plants. She likes to pick them, which means she will shred every one of them."

"You wouldn't do that, would you, sweetie?"

"Do at."

"Where's the hunk this morning?" Amanda settled back with the baby perched on her lap. "I've been dying to ask how it's been going."

Before Holly could formulate an answer, one of the Masterses' housekeeping staff called to her. "Ms. Anderson?" A tall, elderly man accompanied by a postal employee walked toward where they sat.

"Hey, Holly," Joe Green said. "Chance has a certified letter from the US Department of Defense. Can you sign for it? Do you know when he'll be back?"

"I don't even know where he went." Chance had already been gone when she'd woken up around eight o'clock. She hadn't knocked on his door, but she felt relatively certain he would have made an appearance by now if he was still around the house. She'd assumed he was down at the barn.

"Commander Masters rode his horse out to see his mother's house," the butler said. "I will find someone to take the letter to him. It might be important."

Holly sent a quick glance to Amanda and received a nod. She held her hand out for the electronic confirmation of receipt. "I'll take it to him. I know about where his mother's house is."

"Sections of the road have flooded in the past. As I understand, even a Jeep can't travel the old road that Mrs. Masters used to use."

She nodded and looked at the white envelope in her hands. This was it. This had to be what Chance had been waiting for. A decision had been made as to whether he could return to active duty. She just knew it. Holly was suddenly bombarded with emotions that hit her from every direction. She'd known this was coming. She thought she'd steeled herself from feeling anything other than happy for Chance, but that tiny hole in her heart began to emerge.

She rose from the chair, the letter clutched

tightly in her hand. Emma was still contentedly sitting on Amanda's lap. She gave Emma a big hug and kiss.

"Thanks, Mandy."

"This is it? He's leaving?"

Holly glanced at the letter in her hand. "I have no way of knowing for sure, but that would be my guess."

She ran into the house and changed into jeans and a clean shirt. Her heart was beating as though she'd run a marathon. She grabbed the letter and forced herself to smile as she passed through the flagstone courtyard and waved goodbye to Amanda and Emma. In the barn she went straight for Sin. She wanted a mount she could absolutely trust. Positioning the blanket on his strong back, she threw a Western saddle on top, quickly adjusting it before tightening the cinch. Rather than his eggbutt snaffle bit, she chose a Western headstall from the tack room. The sky was becoming dark and thunder rolled across the sky in the distance. She had no way of knowing what she would face. It was a long ride.

Swinging into the saddle, she headed to the

gate that opened to the northern acres. Leaning forward, Sin took the cue and immediately set off in a canter, his dark gray mane and tail flying out behind him.

Chance sat on the front porch of the small cabin as the memories continued to wash over him. It had been so many years ago that he'd stood next to his mother watching as the house was built. He'd sensed something was wrong, but being just a kid he probably wouldn't have understood it if she'd taken the time to explain it to him. His mother hadn't lived for riches and social status. She'd lived for the love of her husband. And after waiting for years for him to return that love, she'd finally given up. Who was she to compete with the elation in his face when he had again succeeded in buying out yet another company, increasing both his reputation as a highly successful businessman and his wealth? In Chance's father's eyes, nothing could compare with that.

She'd brought to her new house only the things she'd brought into the marriage and not a lot else, other than pictures of her children and a few souvenirs of happier times. She'd loved art. Drawing and painting had been her passion and she was good. Sadly no one had ever seen her talent. Except Chance. He'd asked her once why she didn't sell her paintings or display them in a gallery. He remembered her sad smile when she'd shrugged and said they were worth something only to those who appreciated art. "I paint them because I enjoy it, not to sell for money," she'd said. It was years later he'd realized what she meant. They were not Rembrandts or painted by Michelangelo or da Vinci. So in his father's eyes they had been worthless. The hours she'd spent painting was time forever lost.

The thunder rumbled overhead and Chance noticed the darkening sky. He'd better get back to the ranch. Maybe his commanding officer had returned his phone call. Hell, maybe he'd even called to give Chance some good news. And maybe pigs would start flying tomorrow.

He rose from the small chair and headed around to the back of the house where a small barn and corral had been built. The big bay nickered at him, a clear indication it was ready to go home.

Quickly saddling the horse, he mounted and headed south. He hadn't gone far when the first drops of rain made a light tapping sound on the brim of his hat. Before he'd gone a mile the rain increased to a steady downpour. He took the gelding into a canter. Rain had never bothered him but the ground was beginning to move—a sure sign of flooding. Just ahead was the river. The water was running fast and rising. He considered the best place to cross and in that moment he saw something at the river's edge some distance ahead. A gray horse was standing with its front feet in the river, pawing at something in front of him on the ground. As Chance got closer he saw it was a person.

He urged the bay into a flat-out run. The closer he got the more he felt fear. It was a feeling he'd not previously experienced, but there was no shaking it. And the closer he got the worse it grew. It was Holly. He was certain of it. She lay on her stomach, her head toward the rising water. What had happened? Was she alive?

He jumped from the saddle before the horse had a chance to come to a complete stop.

"Holly? Baby, can you hear me?" He knelt next to her on the soaked earth. When she didn't answer, something close to panic gripped his throat. "Holly."

He heard a small moan. Then remarkably, she moved her arm under her and attempted to push up.

"Take it easy, sweetheart," he said. "Try not to move. Can you tell me where you're hurt?"

His SEAL medical training kicked in, and thank goodness for that. Once he was sure she was relatively unharmed, he helped her sit up. She was groggy after apparently having the breath knocked out of her. Sin nickered and tried to push Chance out of the way. The rain was still coming down.

"Holly, we've got to get you to a dry place. I'm going to pick you up. Tell me if it hurts anywhere." He saw her nod her head. As Chance drew her into his arms, she made no sound. But he wouldn't know with any certainty if she was okay until he got her to his mother's house, where he could check her more attentively. With Holly in his arms, he walked toward the gelding.

"Wait. The letter. Must find the letter." She spoke in a whisper. It was hard to understand what she was saying. He felt her take a deep breath. "The letter. Chance, I won't leave until I find the letter."

What letter?

"Holly, this storm is building and about to kick our butts."

She tried to push out of his arms. "Let me down. Chance, put me down. I've got to find the letter."

He didn't understand what could possibly so be so important that she would risk her life. But he set her on the ground.

"Just stay there, I'll go look." He walked back to the spot where he'd found her, and sure enough there was a white envelope half covered in mud. He picked it up, slung off most of the mud, folded it so that he could shove it into his back pants pocket, then he ran back to Holly.

"I found it. I've got the letter. Now let's get you out of here."

She nodded. "I can ride. I just got the breath knocked out of me when Sin fell coming up the side of the embankment. Is he all right?"

"He seems fine."

When Chance didn't move, she added, "I'm all right. Go. Get your horse." She was now yelling to be heard over the wind and thunder. Chance lifted Holly onto the saddle. As he approached the bay, the lightning crackled overhead and the horse flinched and began to back up. Chance swung out his arms and managed to catch the reins. With a few calming words, he leaped into the saddle and maneuvered the horse toward Holly and Sin.

"You're okay?"

She nodded.

"I don't think we have time to make it back to the ranch," Chance said. "I think we should head for Mom's cabin. It's not far from here."

Holly nodded her agreement. "Lead the way."

As soon as Chance cleared the tall, rocky up-hill grade and reached level ground, he pulled his mount to a stop and waited for Holly and Sin to make it up the rocky hill from the river below.

"Ready?" she asked when she caught up to him.

"It's this way. Let's go." Gathering the reins, he headed back to his mother's small cabin.

The thunder continued to roll across the sky. It was so dark, it looked like midnight. The wind picked up. They were in for a whale of a storm. Only a couple of hours earlier, it had been a bright sunny day with not a cloud in the sky. Typical Texas weather. If you don't like it, stick around a couple of minutes. It will usually change.

Holly urged Sin into a gallop. The thunder became louder, streaks of lightning hitting the ground all around them. The faster they went, the harder the rain stung Holly's face. They had to traverse about a mile of open range before once again entering a tree line. His mother's small house sat some distance deeper into the forested area. Entering the thickening trees, Holly slowed, allowing Sin to pick his way over fallen branches and around thornbushes.

"There." Chance pointed ahead.

Holly could just catch glimpses of the blue roof

almost hidden behind the trees. Chance guided them into the clearing around the house and into a small barn slightly to the left and behind the cabin. Jumping down, he pushed open the tall double doors and motioned for Holly to go inside. Compared with the main barn at the Masterses' ranch, this was tiny. At some time in the past one of the six stalls had been converted to a feed-and-tack room. It appeared fresh bedding had been spread in the stall floors, the individual water troughs filled with fresh water.

"Somebody knew we were coming." Holly laughed and slid down from Sin's back.

"I think the foreman keeps this area fairly clean for just what happened to us today. The storms come on fast. This is about the halfway mark between the house and the butte with the views, where most guests eventually wind up."

After riding up under the protective covering, Chance began to unsaddle his gelding and Holly followed suit with Sin. Everything needed a chance to dry out. Holly led him into the closest stall and removed his saddle, blanket and the headstall. With a good shake of his massive body, Sin dried himself off.

"I think there is some hay at the far end. You might check and make sure it's fresh."

Holly headed in that direction and sure enough, five bales of hay had been set in the corner. Breaking apart one of the bales, she checked for any sign of mold. All was good. She grabbed a couple blocks of the bale and tossed them into Sin's stall before going back for more for Chance's gelding.

While Chance took care of the tack, Holly stood in the structure's opening. The rain was still coming down in heavy torrents. A glance up at the charcoal sky made her wonder if they were going to be bedding down in the other stalls. As a kid, she'd slept in worse. The image came to mind of her huddled next to Chance in the hollow of a giant hickory tree, listening for signs that the black bear had come back. But she'd never felt true fear. Not when Chance was there with her. But being stuffed in that tree hollow had made it a very long night.

"Let's go," Chance said, coming up from behind her.

"Where?"

"In the house."

This was where his mother had lived the last years of her life. It was a special place. Holly hesitated, thinking it might be better if she just remained on the porch.

"If there is a blanket, I'll be fine out here."

His dark brows drew together in a frown. "Holly, it's fine. Come inside. You need to get out of those clothes. We're both soaked."

She looked at Chance long and hard before finally nodding her head in agreement. She'd been very young when his mother died but she remembered the deep grief that had plagued him for weeks—no, months. She'd once overheard Wade ask Chance where he'd been for three days. He'd said, "Mom's house." It was a two-word answer that had been tossed to his brother as he'd walked past him headed to the barn.

"You can't find her there, Chance. You need to accept she's gone and get over it." For the first time Holly had witnessed Chance lose it. He'd had his eldest brother on the ground, his fist slamming his face in less than a heartbeat. Some ranch hands had pulled him off. With one last glare at his brother, Chance had disappeared into the barn. Instinct had warned Holly that it wasn't the time to approach him. She remembered the haunted look that covered his features, the straight line of his mouth, the dead look in his eyes. He'd disappeared shortly after. He'd reported to the Naval Special Warfare Center in Coronado, California, and she'd never seen him again. Until two weeks ago.

He broke into her reflections. "Holly?"

"Yeah. I'm coming."

Holly knew that even after all these years the memories would be as fresh as if the events had occurred yesterday. Though he tried to hide it, she could feel his pain and regret at losing his mother at such a young age. And the anger at his father for contributing to her sadness and consequently, her early demise, stirred the anguish in Chance's heart.

Inhaling a deep breath and blowing it out, Holly walked to the front door and stepped inside.

Eleven

The house was small, especially when compared with the mansion on the hill, but she could see how Chance's mother could be comfortable here. Raised ceilings made it feel a lot bigger than it probably was. The kitchen with granite counter-tops and oak cabinets opened into the den. Frilly curtains hung over the windows. The four canis-ters on the counter intended for flour, sugar and such were shaped mushrooms, with small bright orange spotted mushrooms painted on the sides and lids. It was colorful, bright and cheerful.

Holly walked through the house at a leisurely pace. The bedrooms each had an accent wall painted in a cheery color of blue, yellow or green, the decor just as delightful as the kitchen's. *Whimsical.* That was the word. The entire house was whimsical. And she loved it.

"Okay if I take a shower?" The force of the storm was increasing. It would be a while before they were able to return to the ranch. She could feel the dried mud on her face.

"Of course. Help yourself."

The robe she found in a bedroom closet must have belonged to his mother. After taking a quick shower, she reentered the den. The robe fit perfectly. She set her dirty clothes on the kitchen floor, spreading them so they would dry a little bit. Chance had a small fire going in the fireplace. She couldn't help but notice he still wore his wet jeans but his shirt had been removed and lay on the floor of the kitchen.

"There's a washer and dryer in a utility room behind the kitchen. You can dry your things there."

"Okay. What about your jeans?"

"I'm fine."

"No, you're not." Holly held out her hand, palm

up, her fingers waving in a gesture of "give them here." "Give."

"I don't think that's a good idea."

"You need dry clothes." She tilted her head, defying him to argue with logic. When Chance didn't respond, she said, "Now who's suddenly playing Mr. Modest? Sounds like a dare is needed. Let's see…"

"You are just about the most ornery woman I've ever met in my entire existence."

"Funny. That's exactly what I say about you. Give me your pants."

Shaking his head, he headed for the bathroom. A few minutes later he poked one hand outside the door and dumped his muddy clothes onto the floor.

"I'm covered in mud. Gonna take a shower."

Holly grabbed his jeans, picked up his shirt and her clothes and headed for the laundry room. Every article of clothing was caked with mud. If she didn't wash them, they would be ruined. Tossing everything into the washer, she added the detergent and hit the button. She returned to the den just as Chance was adding a couple of logs to the fire. He'd found an old pair of jeans from somewhere. The warmth spread out into the room, giving it a cozy, inviting feeling.

Holly idled around the room. In one corner a painting of the three Masters brothers sat on an easel.

"Did your mother paint this?"

"Yeah."

She had captured each of their characters beautifully. Wade, the eldest, with that stern, in-charge face even when he was about fifteen. Something about the brown eyes softened his features, making him appear a little less arrogant. The picture showed his strength and determination. Confidence. He was very much in charge. Next to Wade was Cole, the middle son. At fourteen, he had a straightforward grin and his honey-brown eyes sparkled. He'd always had the tendency to see the humor in the world. He never appeared to take anything all that seriously, a trait that duped a lot of people. He was as sharp and cunning as a fox, something business adversaries discovered after it was too late.

Holly had heard Cole was one hell of a negotiator. She had no reason to doubt it.

Then there was Chance, the playboy of the three: the impossibly handsome bad boy, adorable even at the tender age of ten. All of the brothers had had their fair share of women ogling them since they'd reached adolescence, but from what her brother told her, Chance had latched on with both hands. Once again, Elaine had captured him perfectly. There was a distinct difference between Chance and his brothers. His vivid blue eyes glowed in contrast to their brown. His hair was a bit lighter in color. Even so long ago, Chance had been unique.

"There is coffee in the kitchen," he said. "On the counter to the right of the sink. The cups are in the cabinet above it."

"Thanks."

When she came back with her steaming brew, Chance reached out to his own coffee cup he'd set on the edge of the stone hearth. He took a sip and put it back down, never taking his focus off the letter in his hand. Suddenly, with the small fire blazing behind him and his face drawn in concentration, she was looking at Lieutenant Commander Chance Masters, US Navy SEAL. Serious. Strong in both mind and body. Of above-average intelligence with a physique to back up any immediate, life-threatening decisions he made. It must have been how he'd looked planning his team's next mission down to the last detail. They counted on him and he was there for them.

He always would be.

He was being summoned to California for the final decision by the medical evaluation board. Chance didn't know if that was a good thing or not. He had assumed they would just send a letter notifying him he was either in or out. Apparently they wanted to do it in person.

"So is that your clearance? The news you've been waiting for?"

Holly stood next to him. Seeing her in his mom's robe did odd things to his gut. She was so beautiful with her long hair unbraided so it could dry, the golden waves falling over her shoulders. He couldn't imagine any other woman doing justice to that robe. From the sexiest of negligees to nothing at all, he'd seen everything. No other woman could compare with the vision of Holly he was seeing right now.

"The letter?" she prompted.

"Ah, kinda. I've been asked to appear at a final hearing in front of the medical evaluation board in three days. I guess I'll find out then."

"So after all of this waiting, you get to wait more. That is so unfair."

"Sounds like you're trying to get rid of me," he joked. Holly apparently didn't take it that way. He saw her blink her beautiful eyes in rapid succession before she turned away.

"Don't be silly," she said as she walked to the kitchen. "What do we have in here to eat?"

Holly rarely showed signs of an appetite. Grabbing a piece of cheese or a carrot and eating while on the go had always been her MO. She was upset. She was upset about the letter and what it meant.

"Holly," he said, getting to his feet. He could see how she was fighting to maintain the thin sliver of control as a battle raged within her.

"Got any peanut butter?" She opened a cabinet, closed it and moved to another one. She grabbed the small jar of Peter Pan and lowered it from the shelf, turning it round and round in her hands. He knew her mind was a thousand miles away. In Coronado.

"Holly," he said, leaning over her, his arms on either side, balancing his weight on the counter. "I'll come back. Even if I'm cleared for duty, I swear I will come back." Coming back to the ranch was not a promise he wanted to make, but it was a promise he would keep. For Holly. If Wade gave them time.

He saw her nod and brush her hand against her cheeks.

"Come on, Holly. Turn around and tell me you believe me."

"I believe you," she said but didn't turn to face him.

Damn. He couldn't do this anymore. He could not deny them what they both wanted. The muscles in his body tightened as the idea took hold, and before he could talk himself out of it, he grabbed her shoulders, turned her around and cupped her face in his hands. "I will come back." He leaned toward her and their breaths fused into one as his lips covered hers, their tongues mating until she sighed and her exquisite feminine body melted into his.

Holly opened her mouth wider, giving him as much as she got, and his body surged to readiness as the kisses deepened and grew more impassioned with every breath. His hands encircled her waist and he set her up on the kitchen counter.

With the ease of experience, he parted her legs, opening them wide enough to accept his girth. Then he stepped up to fill the space. One hand cupped her face, caressing the velvet softness of her cheek. His other hand reached behind her and pulled her forward to the edge of the countertop, nestling his erection at the apex of her thighs. She made a sound somewhere between a sigh and a moan and moved against him. He felt the heat between them scorch like fire and her body went limp. She grabbed the belt loops on his jeans, holding him to her as she pressed harder against his throbbing shaft.

Hell. He wanted to say no. He wanted to stop this before it changed everything, before it could never be taken back. He wanted to ask her if she was sure. But he did none of those things. Instead, he scooped her up into his arms and walked into the bedroom, kicking the door closed behind them.

Settling her gently on the bed, he felt almost disconnected with what was happening. They had denied the passion growing between them for so long, to know what was about to happen felt surreal. The thought of it increased the fire in his loins, his erection throbbing.

"Be sure this is what you want." Was that his voice? So deep and demanding with more than a hint of frantic worry that she would say no. "Because in about three seconds there will be no turning back."

She looked up at him, her eyes soft and clouded, her lips swollen and moist from his kisses. A fierce possession gripped him.

"One. Two. Three," she said. "Take off your jeans."

Chance unsnapped the button on his waistband

and lowered the zipper. Then, bending over her, he parted the robe. Drawing back, he let his eyes roam over her. Holly was so perfect; her skin was so fair, like a porcelain doll. Her breasts were full and heavy, the light pink tips fully erect. Chance lowered himself to suckle one pale rose tip while his hand kneaded the other, his thumb rubbing and teasing. She inhaled deeply, then moaned and arched her back. Her response told him she needed more, and he was ready to give her what she needed.

But she wasn't ready to take him yet. He kissed her silken skin as he worked his way down her body from her lips to her belly. The dark blond curls at the joining of her legs enticed him to explore what other secrets she was keeping. Pushing her knees apart, he cupped her hips, raising her to him. He had to taste her essence. He wanted to acquaint himself with all of her.

She drew in a deep, long breath when his tongue tasted her for the first time. As he completely enjoyed the silken skin and scent of her, her legs dropped open fully and his erection surged past hard to painful. He was about to lose it, but this had to be for Holly. Suddenly her hands gripped his hair and she stiffened, then cried out. Chance continued to draw out her climax as long as possible, loving the idea he had brought her pleasure. After several minutes she collapsed back on the bed.

Like a wild animal ready to mate, he ditched the jeans and crawled up her body until his swollen shaft was pressing against her. Returning to the succulent nectar of her mouth, he fed, his tongue probing deep before withdrawing, again and again. A slow, increasing beat of pleasure gripped them both.

"Are you ready for me, Holly?"

Her breathing was fast and shallow and she only managed to nod. Her hips pushed against him. "It's so hot…there."

"It's about to get a lot hotter." He smiled at her through the darkness. Removing a silver patch from inside his wallet, he tore it open and slipped the condom on. With his hand, he positioned his heavy erection at her core. She was so wet. And she was right about the heat. He couldn't remember ever being so turned on by a woman.

He wanted to take her hard, give in to the lust that gripped him, sink into her womanhood, feel her grip him with her silky wet core and send them both to the moon. Some sixth sense axed that idea. She was small of stature and he didn't want to hurt her. Slowly, inch by excruciating inch, he entered her, his hands fisted to maintain control. Suddenly, she grew very tight inside and cried out, pushing at his shoulders. All movement stopped. He drew back and their eyes locked. He saw her look of discomfort and was shocked. This was not happening.

"Holly, tell me you've had sex before."

She shook her head. "I never wanted anyone but you. There was no one else I felt drawn to. No one I wanted to be with. Please don't be mad."

His nostrils flared; his jaw clamped down so hard it was sheer luck his teeth didn't shatter from the force. For a second he considered pulling out before it was too late. Even through the shock, he was still highly aroused. She'd saved herself for him. She had never been with another man. Holly moved her hips, pushing up and against him and hurting herself in the effort. It would take more than that. It would require him to do his part. Another look into her beautiful face and Chance knew he would see this through.

He cupped her face in his hands, drawing the sweetness from her lips. "There will be a sharp, deep pain, sweetheart. But it won't last long. I'll do everything I can to make it pleasurable for you."

"Its okay, Chance. I want this. I want you."

Lowering his face to hers once again, he kissed her gently, gradually building back up to the passion of moments ago. When he felt she was ready, he pushed in all the way. Her single cry was swallowed by his mouth.

It was done.

There was a feeling of euphoria, and his passion could no longer be held in check. She was frantic and sexier than ever as he poured every bit of his experience and expertise into making this moment a good memory for her. Then she embraced him, sobbing, panting and crying out his name. Her climax ignited the spark that sent him over the top and beyond. It went on and on until finally, fighting for breath, he pulled her head to his shoulder, his arms holding her against him.

"Holly?" he said, kissing her neck and jaw where it was still moist from their passion. "I need to know that you're all right."

Through the ambient light of the passing storm, he saw her smile. "Wow." She raised her head and kissed him. "Thank you, Chance," she whispered against his lips.

Silence filled the room. The only sound was Holly's soft, steady breathing and the guilt that screamed in his head. Who would have thought Holly would still be a virgin? Chance wasn't sure what to do. This was a first for him. But his protective instincts were on full alert. He would do what was needed to protect her, to keep her safe even from her own heart. She was his. Totally and completely. A fierce pride rumbled through him. But it didn't stop him from remembering there were issues preventing them from being together. Issues he had no clue how to solve.

She ran a veterinarian clinic and was raising a baby. He was a SEAL and never had any intentions of doing anything else. He didn't want a wife to go through three-quarters of the year alone, waiting for her husband to come back, hoping he would. When he came home, he couldn't tell her where he'd been or what he'd been doing. With any luck, he would have a few months before he'd be gone again. Sometimes not that long.

It was an impossible situation. Wade was selling the ranch. If Chance wasn't cleared to active duty, what would he do? He'd never been the type to sit around on his ass.

Lightning flashed and Holly snuggled closer. He'd never held a woman after sex. Once he and a date got what they'd come together for, one of them always left with an "I'll call you" thrown over a shoulder on the way out the door. He had to admit, holding Holly, the way she was curled up in his arms, felt good. He could get used to this.

This was all too crazy. Something had to give. He just didn't know what.

When Chance awoke the next morning, Holly was already up. There were mouthwatering smells coming from the kitchen. He headed for the bathroom. When he came out from taking his shower, his clean clothes were laid out on the mattress. The bedding had already been stripped and was no doubt in the wash.

Shuffling into the kitchen, he saw Holly was frying bacon and eggs. Her back was to him. He went to her and put his arms around her. She turned in his arms and pulled him down to her. No words were needed as she stood on her tip-toes and kissed him.

Then drawing back, she said, "There's fresh coffee. I didn't know if you took cream or sugar. The sugar is next to the coffeepot. If you need cream, you'll have to find a cow." By the time he poured a steaming cup of black coffee, she was setting the bacon, eggs and toast on the table.

"Holly," he began as he pulled out a chair. "About last night—"

"No. We are not going to do the guilt-trip thing. It happened. It was beyond wonderful. I don't expect anything from you and I'm not asking for anything. Now eat your eggs before they get cold."

"I don't want to let this drop. Last night was special, but you should have told me you were a virgin."

"Why?" she asked, pouring a cup of coffee with a steady hand. "Would you have done something different?"

"Maybe."

She rose from her seat, leaned over and gave him a kiss full of passion edged with temptation. "I don't think a first time can get any better. Thank you, Chance."

Chance still didn't feel right about taking her virginity. Hell, he hadn't intended to make love to her, but as usual with Holly, things had gotten out of hand. All he knew to do now was keep a close watch on her, be alert for any signs of regret and be there for her if any remorse made its presence known.

"Now eat your eggs before they get cold."

He closed his mouth and realized it had been gaping open. "Yes, ma'am." And he attacked the best breakfast he'd ever had. Somehow, from Holly, he expected nothing less.

Twelve

The clinic was back in business and playing catch-up. With the new equipment installed, they had never been busier, which was a good thing for lots of reasons. The number one reason was because it kept her busy. Holly didn't have time to dwell on what had happened with Chance. He'd made it clear he wanted her then and forever but on the heels of that, he'd left for his hearing and wasn't sure when he would be back.

Holly didn't know what to expect after they made love. Obviously they had taken their relationship to an entirely new level, but they hadn't worked out how to overcome the barrier between them. Probably because there was no answer.

Holly never thought it was possible to love anyone as deeply as she loved Chance. She knew he wasn't the type to settle down, marry and raise a family. If that had changed, he could find somebody a lot better than her. Someone who could give options of whether or not he wanted kids, where they lived and how they wanted to enjoy their life together. She couldn't offer him any of those things. She had a clinic and couldn't walk out and leave Kevin holding the bag. She had pledged her help just as he'd promised her the same. And she had a baby girl to raise. A very special, very beautiful baby girl. And even if Chance actually asked her to come with him, she would have to say no. It was his life, the one he'd chosen. It was not hers. That was something she couldn't let herself forget, regardless of how much she wanted to be with him. Regardless of how much she loved him.

She knew that his hearing had been scheduled for yesterday at 1:00 p.m. No phone call yet. What could that mean?

She finished the last farm call around four that afternoon and she still didn't want to go home. She knew when she did she would feel Chance's absence as she had every day since he left. Emotionally it had been a very difficult week and she was still on pins and needles. Would they reinstate him or set him free?

Amanda had taken Emma to visit her parents, promising to have the baby home by six. Holly didn't know how, but she'd swear that Amanda knew something had happened between her and Chance. Was Holly that transparent? She supposed it didn't matter that Amanda was suspicious. She appreciated her friend's help and understanding.

She'd overheard Cole tell the general manager of the ranch he didn't think Chance was coming back. But Chance had promised he would. She believed him because not believing Chance was unthinkable.

It was the scream from a wild mustang that shattered the evening calm. Eight of them had been brought to the ranch to be trained and cared for with the hope of finding each a good home when the rehabilitation was done. But there was so much public outcry that their population was increasing too fast, doubling every four years and wreaking havoc. Ranchers in the area claimed the damage done to the open government grass-lands prevented others from using it for feeding their livestock. There was talk of thinning out the herd by any means available. That meant rifles. That meant innocent horses would die.

The Circle M was one of many ranches to be-come involved with saving the mustang. It had joined with other ranches in an effort to bring the wild horses back for rehabilitation. For four years crews from the ranch had journeyed to New Mexico and Arizona a couple of times a year. The results so far had been good.

The office door burst open. Amanda's eyes were wild as though in shock. "Is Emma with you? Do you have her?"

"No," Holly answered as a bolt of pure fear shot down her spine.

"She was standing just inside the office door. I stopped to talk to Kenneth and apparently

Emma ventured back outside. I can't find her. Anywhere."

Holly burst into a dead run, heading for the holding pens and calling over her shoulder for Amanda to go to the barn.

Chance stepped out of the chopper, thanking the pilot for the ride. As soon as it was airborne again, he walked to the nearest holding corral, watching while the cowboys separated the mares from the stallions. In this bunch that had just come in, there was only one male. And it appeared he wasn't going to go quietly. Finally, in a combined effort, he was separated from the rest and placed into another pen by himself. He was not happy. A few days to settle down and he would start the long training process. Chance wished he could be here to help. But he had other battles to fight, namely the war against the terrorists in Afghanistan.

He'd been reinstated. He should be doing backflips. But he was grim. He'd done a lot of thinking over the past few days. For all his SEAL training, he hadn't come up with a solution to keep Holly in his life. Being back on the ranch, he felt the situation was as hopeless as when he'd left. He hadn't wanted to tell her over a phone. And he hoped she might have some idea, regardless of how crazy, that would let them stay together. For the first time in his life, Chance was ready to say "I do" and afraid she would say "I don't." Slapping his gloves against his leg, he walked toward the house.

He hadn't gotten very far when he heard a woman calling Emma's name. As the tension in her voice grew more and more frantic, it immediately made Chance go on full alert. Out of the corner of his eye he saw Holly running toward Amanda like the devil himself was on her tail. Why would Holly's friend, Amanda, be calling Emma as though she didn't know where she was? Chance stopped. That sixth sense he'd always relied on had the hairs on the back of his neck standing straight up. Something was wrong. He turned around and started jogging back to the barn. Then Holly took off, running toward the other side of the barn where the mustangs were being kept. She was running frantically in circles, now screaming Emma's name.

He caught up with her, his hands holding her shoulders as he tried to understand what was wrong. She was almost hysterical.

"Holly, talk to me. Where is Emma?"

"Chance? You're here?" She fell into his arms before pushing back. "We can't find Emma. I got a call from Jim Dugan, your ranch manager, asking me if I could please come up and take a look at the new batch of mustangs and see if I can spot anything that needed immediate attention. I was in his office and Emma was standing next to me. Amanda had just brought her inside. The door was closed. The next thing we knew she was gone."

"Okay. Try to calm down. We'll find her."

"How could she have gotten out of that room without me seeing her?" Then, as though she realized talking about what happened was wasting time, she once again started screaming for the baby. Her face was red, her eyes swollen and it appeared shock was settling in.

In between the screams Chance heard something. It sounded like an infant's laughter. Where was she? She couldn't be far. Apparently Holly had heard it, too. Her frantic calls stopped and she, too, was trying to home in on where the laugh had come from. Chance watched as Holly walked toward the holding pens on the west side of the barn. She paused. Seconds later she was screaming again. This time it was his name.

Chance ran toward her faster than humanly possible. From the direction Holly was looking he knew the only thing she saw were the pens that contained the wild mustangs. As he reached Holly, one glance told him the little kid was in big trouble. Emma was holding up her hand, clinching what looked like some grass. And she was offering it to the mustang stallion.

Like a crazed person, Chance took off for the baby, fear tearing down his spine, closing his throat and shutting down his mind to all but one thought: get to Emma before the mustang did. In his mind he was back in Iraq commanding his body to make up those three seconds. Another tiny life rested in his hands, and that thought turned to pure adrenaline. He would not let another child die needlessly. He would not let Emma be hurt.

He cleared the six-foot-high fence as though it didn't exist. About the time he landed on the other side, the stallion had seen the baby. She was still walking toward it holding up the grass in her hand. The mustang's ears were flat against its head as it pawed the ground and bared its teeth, all signs of imminent attack. There was a distance of about ten feet between the mustang and Emma. The horse could lurch that far in one stride. Chance had to run faster, harder. He needed those three seconds.

The situation played out in slow motion with every sinew in his body straining to go faster. Chance caught the baby in his arms, never breaking stride. He jumped up onto the fence on the east side just as the stallion pounced. Knowing it missed its target, it first reared up, then wheeled around and kicked the fence, the strike landing less than a foot away from where Chance held the baby.

By now the cowboys had heard the commotion and were coming out to help. When he jumped down on the outside of the fence, Emma's head was against his shoulder, her little arms around his neck, and nothing he'd ever experienced in his life had ever felt so great.

He walked toward Holly, who was running to him.

"Hoshee!" Emma exclaimed, giggling.

"Yeah," Chance answered. "Bad hoshee. Emma stay away from that hoshee. Okay?"

"Bah hoshee."

He handed her to Holly, who hugged her as though she never wanted to let her go. Tears were flowing down her cheeks.

"Thank you, Chance. Oh, my gosh. *Thank you.*"

As she hugged him to her, the baby turned in her arms and was patting his chest. "Ta you." And Chance hugged them both.

Holly paced the floor. The incident with Emma had shaken her up so badly her heart hadn't slowed down even two hours after it happened. Amanda had offered to take Emma back to her parents, but Holly refused to let Emma out of her sight. She would have nightmares for a very long time after what had happened. She and Amanda had talked and neither could understand how the baby had gotten out the office door, walked all the way across the private road and into the pen with that mustang. Thank God for Chance. Emma could have been dead right now. Holly couldn't even get her mind around that. She owed Chance more than she could ever repay.

But what was he doing here? She knew his hearing had been scheduled for yesterday afternoon. She'd been waiting for the phone call that never came. Then suddenly he'd shown up in time to save her baby. She didn't know what to make of it. She thought about going to the big house and asking him. But in addition to the fact she was still trembling over Emma's close call, she believed if Chance wanted her to know the outcome of his hearing he would tell her. It wouldn't make the answer different if she went over and beat on his door, although that was exactly what she wanted to do.

Lightning flashed in the distance. Standing at the window, Holly wished this nightmare could be over. Chance would be leaving. She felt it. The doctor here had given him a clean bill of health, saying the wounds were healing nicely. That was a good thing. The medical evaluation board had probably decided in his favor and allowed Chance to go back to his team. She and Emma would continue their lives and maybe, someday, Chance would come back. He still loved the ranch. Maybe if he retired from the military he would come here to live out his life.

As the thunder rolled in, she continued to pace. She hated waiting for something to happen once it was a done deal. She had learned the hard way she was lousy at saying goodbye. Ironically Chance was always the one she was saying goodbye to. While she didn't want Chance to leave—ever—if he was going to she wanted it over with. Counting down the hours and minutes until he boarded the plane and left her was tying her insides into knots. A tear broke loose and fell down her cheek. Absently she brushed it away. Only to have it replaced by another.

She really needed to stop this. She'd accepted that Chance would never stay. It was so stupid of her to have her own little pity party like this. She walked into the bathroom and grabbed a section of tissue to blow her nose and wipe her eyes.

Someone knocked on her back door. *Please don't let somebody have an emergency tonight.* She was almost to the door when the knocking came again. She realized she was wearing only an oversize T-shirt and her panties. "Give me just a minute," she called out, and scurried to put on a pair of jeans. Then she came back and cracked open the door just enough to see who was there.

"Holly?" It was Chance.

Had he come to say goodbye? He must have really wanted her to know he was leaving to show up in person at midnight.

"I know you're leaving," she whispered through the crack in the door. "You didn't have to stop by and tell me in person, but thank you. And I can never thank you enough for saving Emma. Please take care of yourself. Okay?"

A strong gust of wind brought the rain slamming against her house. The tears returned about the same time.

"Holly, let me in."

"No. Chance, you need to go." Yes, she wanted to be in his arms again. But she didn't want to prolong the goodbye.

"I'm not leaving until I make sure you're all right. Until we've had a chance to talk." She heard the determination in his voice and knew he would stand outside in the rain with lightning crackling overhead all night if that was what it took.

With both hands she wiped the moisture from her cheeks and stepped back into the room, letting the door fall open.

Chance stepped inside and closed the door behind him. His eyes were on her face. On the tears that refused to stop falling. "Holly, don't do this."

She turned away from him. "If you don't have an animal emergency…"

He put his hands on her shoulders and spun her around to face him. He should never have come back to the ranch. He'd told her he would call and that was what he should have done. He should never have made love to her knowing full well he would be leaving. He knew her heart.

She lived life, she didn't just walk on the edge of it. Small things that most people didn't notice made Holly laugh for joy. But it worked the other way, too. Things that made others feel a little sad could rip a hole through her heart. She'd lost so much. He had a feeling that in her mind she was losing him, as well.

He loved her. He probably always had. But he couldn't stay. What would he do if he left the military? He just couldn't see himself wearing a suit to work every day and becoming a pencil pusher like his brothers. He was not cut out for that. If he tried to force it, Holly would pay the price by putting up with what she called a grouch.

"Are congratulations in order? Are you going to be reinstated?"

He hesitated, knowing the answer was not what she wanted to hear. "Yes. I leave in the morning to report to the naval base in Coronado."

"Then definitely, congratulations. I'm very happy for you."

She did her best to smile, but he could see the truth in her eyes.

"This, what we have, is not over, Holly. That's why I came back. To tell you, in person, I want you in my life."

She walked to a chair and leaned against the back of it as though she needed the support.

"And what, exactly, do we have, Chance? A childhood full of memories and making love in the rain?" She looked down to where her hands gripped the chair back. "We both know you don't have to come all the way here for that sort of thing. In fact, I'm sure there are plenty of women who have vastly more experience than me who would love to take my place."

He walked toward her. "Make no mistake, Holly. It's you I want." His voice was rough and low even to his own ears. "I want you in my arms, I want to kiss you like there's no tomorrow. I want to bury myself inside you, as deep as I can go. Deeper. I want to tease you about riding English. I want to teach you how to swim. I want it all." He stepped closer. "I want you to come with me. I want to marry you, Holly. Please say yes. I don't know when I'll be back."

The tears swam in her eyes. "I can't, Chance."

"Why?"

"Let's just say I know how to swim and leave it at that, okay?"

"No. We're not leaving it there. I thought...I thought you loved me."

"I do. With all my heart and soul. It would be my dream come true, but eventually reality comes knocking," she said. "You have a team who counts on you, who cares about you. I have patients who need me. And of course, my number one priority is Emma. I'm all she has, Chance."

"I'm not asking you to leave Emma." He frowned, upset that she would ever think such a thing. "I would never do that."

"Chance, please understand what I'm saying. She will never know her mother or father. But at least here, in Calico Springs, she will grow up in a community where they lived. She will meet people who knew them and loved them and she'll hear good things. She'll grow up proud she is Jason's daughter. And they will love her as one of them. I won't take that away from her. It's all I have to give her."

Chance looked into Holly's eyes, and saw her

determination to protect and do what was right for Emma clearly reflected there. He took her into his arms. He needed to hold her, to feel her next to him. He was a bit surprised when she made no effort to push away because clearly she was upset. He bent down and kissed the side of her face. She turned toward him, her lips seeking his. He could taste the salty remnants of her tears.

As always, her lips were so soft. Like the softest velvet he could imagine. As he kissed her he felt the stiffness leave her body, and her arms came around his neck. And she kissed him back as if this was the last time she would ever see him.

Eventually, they pulled apart.

"So I guess this is really it."

"I guess so. We had a good time, didn't we?" She crossed her arms around her as though giving herself some needed support. He could see the tears still falling down her face even as she tried to blink them away. It was so Holly. She'd always been so tough, so determined. Especially when it meant keeping up with her big brother and his friend Chance. Thank heavens that hadn't changed.

"Holly, I keep thinking there is some sort of solution here. The money is there, but I've never been one who could sit on my hands. A few months with me underfoot, you really would be calling me a grouch. And…there's something else you should know. Wade is selling the ranch, so prepare for some new neighbors."

The shock on her face was immediate. "*What? How can he do that?*"

"He is the head of Masters Corporation. The corporation owns the land. He can do anything he wants."

"But the ranch… It was the beginning of all of us. Jason, you, Wade, Cole. It's where your mother is laid to rest. It should be yours. This is so wrong. I'm going over there and light into Wade Masters like…"

"No, Holly," he said. "Wade is doing what he thinks is best. The ranch isn't profitable, and it's too big to try to support it. He will do right by you, Holly. Don't hold it against him." Chance looked around the room as though unsure what his next move should be. "Okay. Well, I'd better get going. I'll be in touch, okay?"

"Sure. You take care and don't get shot again, for gosh sakes." Again she tried her best to smile.

There was nothing else to say. There was no use in prolonging her sadness. Or his.

With a nod to her, Chance turned and walked out the door.

He didn't see Holly double over in pain. He didn't hear the hopeless cries of anguish or her soft but broken voice saying, "I love you, Chance Masters. I always will."

Thirteen

The combined sounds of announcements over the loudspeaker and the disgruntled mooing of cows told Holly the rodeo was well underway. A loud buzzer signaled the end of time for a wild bronc rider. Holly had grown up at these events and she never could quite understand why any man would put his life on the line if he didn't have to. Who in their right mind would try to go eight seconds on a bull with three-foot-long horns and a really bad attitude? Her brother and Chance used to ride those bulls. She'd thought they were crazy then. She still thought it was insane. But she always admired the roping competitions and had won her share of ribbons for the barrel-racing event.

She walked toward the area that had been set up for her use. Next door, another tent, quite a bit larger, had been erected for the area doctor. She loved old Doc Hardy. It was easy to understand why this community refused to let him even think about retiring. He welcomed her with a hug.

"Let's hope neither man nor horse gets injured tonight," he said. "Are you here for both nights, Holly?"

"No, sir," she said. "I've got it tonight. Kevin will be here tomorrow."

"I like that young man. Seems like a hard worker. And his boys were in to see me for preschool inoculations and they are just as nice and respectful as their father. The mother, too."

"I couldn't agree more."

Holly inventoried the medical equipment brought over by members of the Calico County Rodeo Association. As far as she could tell, everything was here. She shared the hope that neither she nor Doc Hardy had to use any of it. Her for the animals. Dr. Hardy for the people.

"Say, Holly. Did you know Chance Masters?"

Her heart plunged to her feet. "Yes. Yes, I did."

"He and your brother were always at the rodeo. I heard he was back in town after a dozen years or more. Can't rightly recall how long. I always wondered what happened to him. The only time he wasn't getting himself in trouble was when he was with Jason. I think your brother put his foot down and wouldn't stand for any of that rabble-rousing. But you know, it might have been a lot different if his father had given two hoots about his sons. I think he was cruel to Chance and Chance finally had enough. A lot of that trouble he caused was because of his father."

"Really?"

"Yeah. Like I said, I always wondered what happened to him. I know there was some good in that boy."

"I heard he is a navy SEAL." Holly volunteered the info, still trying to digest what Dr. Hardy had said.

"Is that right? Good for him. It's like I thought, after his father threw him out of his house there were all kinds of directions he could have gone.

He made the right choice. I'm happy to know that."

It had been three weeks and five days since Chance had walked out of her house and out of her life forever. Thankfully Amanda didn't mention him. Her friend knew Holly's heart was still healing. But it was unexpected inquiries, like Dr. Hardy's, that slipped through her defenses. Those were hard. But she was making progress. She no longer cried herself to sleep every night. And she'd begun eating regular meals, required if she was to do her job. But even she could look in the mirror and see the dark circles under her eyes and a general pallor to her skin. It couldn't be helped. She was doing the best she could.

"I'm going to go and get one of Judy's corn dogs. Would you care for anything, Dr. Hardy?"

"Thank you, Holly, but Martha sent me with a thermos of coffee and a bunch of lettuce and told me I'd better not set my sights on a dessert."

Holly couldn't help but smile. "I'll be right back."

With a couple of cowboys standing watch to ensure her supplies and equipment didn't grow legs and walk off, she strolled through the crowd, looking at the various vendor booths selling everything from tack to Western-related jewelry. But her focus was on Judy Cooper's hot dog stand.

"Hi, Doc." Judy spotted her in the crowd. "I've got that corn dog and homemade lemonade almost ready for you."

"Great." Holly smiled. "It wouldn't be the annual rodeo were it not for your corn dogs."

Leaving a five-dollar bill on the counter, Holly waited for the lemonade to be freshly made.

"Well, hello, stranger. Long time no see."

Holly cringed and turned to face Blake Lufkin. "How have you been doing?"

"Fine. I've been good. How about yourself?"

How long did it take Judy to mix up one glass of lemonade?

"Is that guy you were hanging around with still around?"

"No. He had to go back to his SEAL team. But he will be back." She didn't know if he would or not, but the least Chance could do was be her excuse to keep this irritating man away.

"Here ya go, Holly," Judy said, handing her one dog and a large lemonade.

"Thanks."

"You are entirely welcome." She then turned to Blake. "Can I help you, sir?"

Holly didn't stick around to hear his answer. She was done being nice to the creep. Sipping her lemonade, she made her way back to her medic tent and thanked the cowboys who'd watched it for her.

"Some guy was by here looking for you," Larry offered. "About ten minutes ago. I told him you'd gone to get something to eat and would be back."

"Thanks, Larry."

Great. Now she had people helping the creepy guy track her down.

Holly pulled up a chair toward the front of the tent so she could catch the evening breeze. She had just finished her corn dog and was sipping the last of her lemonade when Blake walked into her tent and pulled up the other chair next to hers as though he had every right to be there.

"Enjoy your food?" he asked. "Frankly, I don't see how you can eat that stuff. How about let's go into town after the rodeo and grab something decent?"

"No, thanks. After the events are over I'll have to get home."

"How about if I come over there? Once you get the kid to bed we could watch a movie. I love the *Mission Impossible* films, so we've got that in common."

Holly was determined to look unimpressed. "I really don't like those kinds of movies."

"I thought I remembered seeing a box full of them next to the TV."

Must belong to Amanda, she mused. Then the deeper meaning of what he'd just said hit her like a blow to the solar plexus. Blake had never been inside her house.

"So how about that dinner? Anywhere you want. Or we could go to my place and see what we can find there." Blake stood up, facing her. He leaned forward, his hands resting on the arms of her chair. Too close. But what she saw made her eyes pop out of her head. He was wearing a pendant. When he leaned toward her it swung forward. And Holly grabbed it. It was a pendant made and given to her by a ten-year-old. It had hung in the clinic.

She saw a moment of surprise in his creepy face. If he left he would destroy the pendant and no one could ever prove he had it. It would be her word against his.

"I love this pendant," she said, making her voice a breathless whisper. "It's beautiful." She looked up into his eyes as though the bastard had walked out of a dream. Heaven help her.

The cut-glass charm depicted a mare and foal in a green pasture. It was one of a kind.

"Oh, Blake." She let her fingers touch the glass. Flipping it over, she found Toby's initials. "I don't suppose the store has any more?" She rose from the chair, purposely standing well within his personal space. Blake had forgotten about the token in her hand, distracted by being this close to Holly. Their faces were inches apart; his breath reeked of alcohol and tobacco, and he generally smelled of someone who hadn't taken a bath in a very long time. She hoped she didn't throw up.

"I'll tell you what. You have dinner with me

and I just might be persuaded to give this little medallion to you. Free."

"Really?" she squeaked, keeping up the dumb blonde persona.

"Well, sure." He went to hug her and she dropped her napkin accidently on purpose.

"Oh, Blake, I have to go find the ladies' room. Oh, I'm so excited. Will you wait for me? Right here? Don't go anywhere. I might not be able to find you." She would probably go to hell for the look of love she plastered on her face.

A disgusting gleam filled his eyes. "Why, sure, Holly. You just take your time. I'll be right here."

She turned after giving him one last smile and stumbled out of the tent. Once out of sight, she ran as if a rabid dog was on her trail. She had to find a deputy, and fast. That necklace had been hanging inside her clinic when it was ransacked. Blake was the culprit.

The crowd parted and just ahead she saw John Green, the deputy who had come out the night the clinic was almost destroyed.

At a dead run she fought to catch up with him. "John. Wait!"

It took two times to make him understand what she was saying. She was panicked that the creep would get away and if that necklace disappeared, they would have no reason to hold him. There might not be any other way to prove he did it.

She made her way back to the tent with John following close behind her. See spotted Blake sitting back in her chair. Unfortunately, he spotted her at the same time. And John Green. Blake was out of the tent, running toward the parking area like the coward he was. Holly refused to let him go and she took after him. After everything he'd put her through, he was going to pay. She heard John calling her name but she wasn't about to stop or slow down.

Blake had disappeared in the parking lot but she had predicted his course. Jumping over parking chains and around bumpers, she managed to get ahead of him, duck down behind a car and wait. Sure enough Blake jogged by, slowing down, obviously thinking he'd lost the cops. He hadn't lost Holly. She put one foot on the bumper to give her leverage and threw herself on top of the man. He was bigger, older, meaner, but she held on. She dug her fingernails into his face and wrapped her legs around his chunky, stinky body. He was cussing, trying to get free. Holly was like an octopus and held on to him with everything she had. They went down in the loose dirt and still she refused to let go. He managed to get on top. She saw the snarl on his face and his fist lift high in the air, and she braced herself for the pain.

But it never came.

She saw strong hands grip Blake's neck and haul the man off the ground.

It was Chance!

Blake took a swing at his captor and Chance flattened him. With one blow. The man was out cold on the ground as John arrived, two deputies in tow.

Offering his hand, Chance helped Holly to stand.

"Well, you damn sure know how to enjoy a rodeo," Chance teased. "The bull riding is on the other side of the fence."

She was covered in dirt from her tussle. She would probably have a couple of bruises, but she didn't care. Chance was here and that creep would soon be behind bars.

"I can't let you out of my sight for an instant," Chance said, trying for a gruff tone but failing miserably. He pulled Holly to him. His lips were on hers, hard, heavy and glorious. In spite of the dirt. In spite of the crowd of curiosity seekers standing around them.

It took her a few minutes to regain her senses. "What…what are you doing here?"

"I missed you, Muppet. I had to come back." His eyes moved over her, top to bottom. "Although I didn't expect to find you rolling around in the dirt with some scumbag."

"That man is the one who ransacked the clinic."

"I hoped he'd done something other than say hello. Let's get you cleaned up."

"The medic tent… I can't leave—"

"Kevin has it all under control. Anyway, another half hour and this rodeo will be one for the history books. In more ways than one. Come on."

The big shower of the en suite room she'd used before when she stayed in the mansion was just what she needed. But she didn't stay under the soothing spray very long. Chance was downstairs. Waiting for her.

She stepped out and grabbed a large towel, wrapping it around her. A quick brush of her hair and she was out the door heading to the den. Chance was in the kitchen, looking into the refrigerator. "Are you hungry?" How had he known she was there?

"Lemonade?"

"Coming up."

She looked at him and it was the most beautiful sight she'd ever seen. And this time she couldn't wait patiently to be told what was happening. "Okay. Tell me why you're here."

He leaned against the kitchen bar, sipping his beer. "I'm here to get married if the beautiful lady I'm in love with still wants me." He set the can down and grew serious. "I quit the SEALs, Holly. It came time to sign up for another three years and I couldn't do it. I looked at the guys I'd served with and I saw your face. And I knew any one of them would call me everything but smart if I didn't get my ass back here and ask you to marry me."

"You're really not going back?"

"Nope. And I'm okay with that. I've done my part."

"What about Emma? You don't like kids."

"I love kids." He was quiet for a moment. "Before we get married, if you agree to marry me, you need to know what kind of man you'll be pledging your life to."

Holly looked at his face. Did he feel as uncomfortable as he looked?

"There is more to it than what it seems. I was in a recon mission. We were provided intel that one of the leading terrorists was in the area hiding out in a small town nearby. We were set to go in, secure the town and capture the guy."

Chance drew in a breath, obviously not wanting to go on. But she had a feeling it was something he needed to say. "At the height of the fighting, a child about Emma's age walked around the corner of a building. She sat down and proceeded to play with this old doll. That's when I saw the bomb coming in fast."

He looked up at Holly, who was frozen in shock. "I hit the ground at a dead run, determined to save her." He ran a hand over his lower face. "I couldn't do it. I couldn't get to her fast enough to save her. The brass wrote it off as collateral damage. But it was the life of a little girl who will never see her second birthday."

"Chance. You can't blame yourself."

"I can and I do. It's reality. It is what it is. I'm afraid of being near your baby because I know someday I might make another mistake. Wait too long. Run too slow. The next time, it might be Emma."

"Chance Masters, you *saved* Emma. Had it not been for you…"

"I got lucky."

"No. What I saw wasn't luck. It was the superhuman effort of a man who cared, determined to save a baby's life. There was no luck involved. And I have no doubt it was the same scene played out when you tried to save the other child."

"You'll have to excuse me if my opinion differs."

Holly didn't know what to say. How could Chance possibly think he was responsible for that baby? But Chance wasn't the kind of man who accepted pity. Anything she said would sound like that to him. At least now she understood why he didn't want to be around babies. She wasn't worried. Emma would fix that.

Holly crossed the space between them, looked up into his face. His eyes said it all. She leaned toward him and placed her arms around his solid waist and her lips against his. He didn't turn her away. Muscles as hard as iron lay beneath her arms. He cupped her face, his rough thumbs rubbing her cheeks. These were the same hands and strong arms that held a rifle with the intent of killing if necessary, if he was ordered to pull a trigger. Now they were so gentle, holding her as he would a baby kitten. He'd put his life on the line every day for his country and dealt with the horror he'd described, carrying it around in his mind. In his soul. It took a very special individual to do that and still go forward.

"I swear, Holly, I'll be the best dad to Emma that I can be."

"I have no doubt of that, Chance," she said, holding him tight. "None."

She felt him inhale as though a weight had been lifted from his shoulders.

"There's one other thing I feel you should know."

Holly waited, not certain what was coming next.

"Wade sold the ranch," he said. "Thought I'd better mention that, too."

She was shocked, but it didn't matter and she wasted no time telling him so. They would find a place of their own.

"I'm so sorry, because I know your love for the Circle M."

Before Holly could wrap her head around that, Chance added, "He sold it to me. We made a deal. It represents my share of the family company. I'll tell you about the particulars some time. But if you will marry me, this will be your home. And Emma's."

"She's gonna love your plants."

"Make love to me." His heavy arms came around her and pulled her tightly against him. With a flick of his wrist, the towel that covered her fell to the floor.

* * *

A soft moan, the sexiest Chance had ever heard in his life, gave him her answer.

She pulled his head down to her, her lips on his, her tongue entering his mouth with a desperate need, giving him all she had to give. And he took it. His hands reached to cover her hips, kneading the firm flesh before he lifted her up and against his throbbing erection. Chance was on fire. The heat that tore through him was burning him alive, and every time she moved the slightest bit his internal thermometer inched up a notch. His hands went to his belt. He had it unbuckled, his jeans unsnapped and his zipper down in seconds. The fact that Holly watched his every movement had the fire once again running through his veins. His jeans fell to his feet. He stepped out of them, tore open the foil packet and put his hands around her waist. He lifted her, positioned his member against her and pushed inside. He was like a wild thing, taking the female he'd chosen as his mate.

Her silver-blond hair splayed out around her head and shoulders. Her eyes were closed, her lips open as she immersed herself in what he was doing. That look of fulfillment brought on the mindless insanity. He didn't want to think. He only wanted to feel, and that feeling was incredible.

Holly's face had always been pretty much an open book and now was no exception. As she opened her eyes, her honey-brown gaze focused on his mouth. It drove him crazy. If she wanted his kiss, he would gladly give her what she wanted. On every square inch of her luscious body.

She brought her silky-smooth legs around him and he began to move. The tension began to build and build until seconds later Holly cried out his name. But he wasn't finished. Not by a mile. Her hands gripped his hair, and she kissed his lips, hungry for anything he could give. And he had plenty he wanted to give. Everything he had was hers.

She was so sensitive, reacting to every touch, every word spoken. How long had he wondered if such a woman existed? Something she said made him break out into a sweat. He felt the familiar tingling in his lower back as his own release overcame him. It seemed to go on and on, every time he heard her saying, "Yes."

Finally, he withdrew from her. Sweeping her into his arms, he carried her to an upstairs bedroom, placed her on the bed and climbed in after her.

Wrapped in each other's arms, they slept. Before morning broke, Holly kissed him awake. She didn't have to tell him why. He grabbed another of the foil packets from the bedside table and took her to the heavens yet again.

Epilogue

Six months later

The small chapel was filled with friends and neighbors who smiled and whispered with hushed excitement about the wedding between two of their own. Who would have ever thought little Holly Anderson would be the one to tame the wild, charismatic, bad-boy billionaire, Chance Masters? Some were here to see it for themselves. Others had already decided they wouldn't believe it regardless of whether they saw it with their own eyes. Some could not contain the pure jealousy evident in their faces. But most were here to see the joining of two people who had loved each other since forever.

The soft strains of a harp combined with the beautiful rhythms of a piano as the front doors opened to allow the bride and her detail to enter. First came two-year-old Emma with her basket of rose petals. Holding Amanda's hand, she walked down the center aisle carefully holding the woven wood basket in front of her. Setting it on the floor, she reached inside and grabbed a handful of petals and dropped them to the floor. After saying hello to the people sitting on both sides, she dutifully picked up the basket, walked another three or four feet, set the basket on the floor and grabbed more petals.

Next to her, the maid of honor, Amanda Stiller, looked behind her to the bride.

"If she doesn't pick up the pace, we are all gonna be here the entire night," Amanda whispered.

Holly grinned at the thought and nodded. She knew Emma would do it her way, so yes, they all might be here for a while. She looked at Emma in time to see her throw down the little basket and run to the front of the chapel, squealing a happy laugh and calling, "Cha, Cha," her little arms held high above her head.

Holly watched as Chance leaned over and picked her up. A lump formed in her throat. They were a family. Chance had overcome his fear he might hurt her and Emma had taken his training over from there. She loved her Cha. Holly caught the radiant blue eyes of her husband-to-be and saw his dimples were showing once again.

I love you, he mouthed.

I love you right back, she mutely answered.

It didn't matter how long the ceremony lasted. She had the rest of her life to love this incredible man. Her hero, her protector, her only love. And she'd make sure he felt that love each and every day for the rest of their lives.

"Emma! Come and get your basket," Amanda said in a loud whisper. "Emma!"

"I'ne get now." Emma wiggled to get down from Chance's arms. She ran halfway down the aisle back to the basket, picked it up and continued to throw the flower petals.

"Good. That's very good," Amanda told her as they made their way to the altar.

And wasn't that the way things were meant to be?

* * * * *

MILLS & BOON®

Why shop at millsandboon.co.uk?

Each year, thousands of romance readers find their perfect read at millsandboon.co.uk. That's because we're passionate about bringing you the very best romantic fiction. Here are some of the advantages of shopping at www.millsandboon.co.uk:

* **Get new books first**—you'll be able to buy your favourite books one month before they hit the shops

* **Get exclusive discounts**—you'll also be able to buy our specially created monthly collections, with up to 50% off the RRP

* **Find your favourite authors**—latest news, interviews and new releases for all your favourite authors and series on our website, plus ideas for what to try next

* **Join in**—once you've bought your favourite books, don't forget to register with us to rate, review and join in the discussions

Visit **www.millsandboon.co.uk**
for all this and more today!